I0710687

The Crimson Scholar

F.L. Journey

ISBN-13: 978-1-965176-05-4

For information please contact publisher at
faireydragonpress@gmail.com

Table of Contents

Dedication

To our parents, for being supportive, even if they don't know what we are doing.

The clanking of metal on stone could be heard reverberating through the large cavern. As the newcomer walked deeper into the cavern, they noticed the sound before anything else. A large stone forge sat in what appeared to be the center of the room. The guest knew this was a room, but the flames threw shadows onto the floor, never reaching the walls. A giant man was wielding a great hammer, and each swing created a thundering sound.

Annoyed at having to wait to speak, the intruder tapped his foot. It created a difficult to ignore cadence between the hammer swings.

"I can hear you, what do you want?" asked the man laboring over the forge as he continued to bring the hammer down in a rhythmic pattern.

"I'm here for the stone I ordered. Is it ready yet, dog?" he yelled over the pounding.

Fenrir rolled his eyes. "First of all, I said I could hear you tapping your foot, so there is no need to yell. One of my gifts is I have great hearing. Second, regarding the stone, no it isn't. You asked for something unique. Stone creation of this caliber isn't something to be rushed."

"Listen here dog, I don't know who you think you are—"

"Well,"—he said, cutting the impatient man off— "Last time I checked, I am Fenrir, son of Loki and Angrboda. Both a god and a wolf." With the last word, Fenrir turned toward the stranger, his face partially transformed into a wolf. Even while in his mostly human form, he was still a full head taller than his visitor. "I have no issues killing you if you continue with your diatribe."

With a smug grin, the stranger walked toward Fenrir, shrouding himself in shadows. "You may try. But you will fail and fail miserably. Within my grasp, I have the full power of the Underworld. Hurt me, and the weight of the Underworld will come crashing down on you." The man stepped from shadow to shadow keeping himself hidden. "You will make that stone for me, and you will make it quickly."

"You have no power over me. However, I said I would create the stone. I would never dishonor myself by leaving a job undone. So, I will finish, but it will be on my time." Fenrir turned completely toward the speaker.

What Fenrir was not about to admit was he had already crafted the red stone. In fact, as with each piece he created, he had poured part of himself into it. Only after creating it did he realize the full potential the stone held. Having a keen sense of others, Fenrir felt something was off about the creature who had requested the stone. Outwardly there was nothing strange, but Fenrir felt malice oozing from the creature's very nature. Not only was the requestor off, but so was the request in itself. Initially Fenrir did not think much of it, but as time went on, the request started to eat at Fenrir.

Fenrir knew he was not who, or what, he said he was. Fenrir prided himself on helping to maintain the balance during the war but not giving one side more power than the other. At least, not until he knew if it would benefit him in some way. He wasn't about to hand over something so powerful to a potential enemy.

"You will finish my stone and give it to me, understand mangy mutt?"

"If you say so." With that, Fenrir turned back to his work, the conversation over. He knew the man was gone, even though he didn't hear him leave. Fenrir wondered if keeping the stone around was a wise choice, especially with how adamant the man seemed to be to acquire it. Looking at the door one more time, Fenrir turned back to the rock he had been working on prior to being interrupted.

It did not matter to him what customers used his creations for. Therefore, he never felt the need to ask. If they shared their intentions, then it would influence his opinion on whether the stone would be used appropriately. Depending on the usage, he may put more or less of himself into making it, and it could change the entire function of the stone. It wasn't that he was the ethics committee. Having a father such as Loki really made him want good in the world versus more chaos. He had mastered an art which allowed him to create objects capable of raining destruction if placed in the wrong hands.

Fenrir couldn't believe his luck when the following week a new customer arrived. While during these times of turmoil he had frequent customers, in peace time it could be years, if not decades, between visitors. So, two in the same number of weeks, while not unusual, was fortuitous for his immediate needs. The new visitor asked for three stones. They were very specific. They wanted each of the stones to bind two souls together, allowing them to communicate telepathically.

The new customer was someone he had known for a long time and could trust. After hearing what she needed, he knew the perfect stone was ready for just this moment. Even if it wasn't going to the original requestor, someone who Fenrir did not trust. Many of its properties would still fit the new request. Sometimes the stone picked the owner, and sometimes the owners are too arrogant. Fenrir could feel this request would be used benevolently. *That is what you get for thinking you could push me argr.*

"Here are your stones, but listen to me carefully," Fenrir spoke as he walked across the cavern, the woman following him. "Keep these protected at all costs. One carries a little more weight than the others. There is no need to tell you which, and it's not something that will hurt the stone carrier. There is power which needs to be used wisely. However, they will all serve your needs."

"Thank you for making the stones. I understand what you are saying, Monster of the River Van."

Fenrir puffed out his chest with pride as he had not been called the moniker in a long time. It was, by far, his favorite nickname. Even though many would consider monster a negative term, Fenrir reveled in it. He was, after all, a monster. Monster in size, monster in bite, monster in growl. "Just remember don't shake the balance."

"By my nature, I strive to be the balance between good and evil. Or at least between good and apathetic. For me apathy can cause more harm than true evil."

"That you are, that you are. Please take the stones and go, but tell no one about the special stone. I do like to keep my trade secrets a secret. And who knows who may come knocking." Fenrir chuckled and moved to his work bench where a small bundle lay, wrapped in animal hide with twine keeping it closed.

Fenrir gently unfolded the hide and handed over three stones, including the little Crimson one he had held near him since its creation. He didn't know exactly how, but he knew the woman clad completely in black would protect the stone with all she had.

"Cee, you have to go to work."

"Why? What's the point? I don't have my dog. I don't have anything. I should go back to school, maybe a distraction will help," Cee said while still watching daytime television in the shared living room.

"Because there are only three of us, and Jan and I both have duties for Hades as well as lives. Not to mention you have pretty much every degree known to man. I mean seriously, what do you have? 10 Doctorates? Now get off your ass and get to work!" Theo now yelled to overpower the volume of the soap opera.

Grunting, Cee stood up, looking over briefly at the stone Doberman. It was placed by the side of the couch as a reminder. A reminder of the missing part of his heart and very soul.

"I just don't know Theo. It's so lonely not having his voice in my head," Cee said, tearing his eyes from the marble statue.

Theo looked at the stone dog before looking over at the Bullmastiff sleeping near the fireplace. "Does this feel different than the short period between companions we normally have?"

For as long as Cee could remember, he had a companion talking away in his head. Over the course of their lives, the brothers had tried to remember how their companions had come to be. Cee was the one who thought about it most of the time, being the scholar, and self-proclaimed historian for the brothers. They only knew they had always been there, both the collars and the companions.

The brothers knew there must have been a time when they did not have the companions, only they had no memory of it. Even with that, it seemed as though their companions had been a part of them since the beginning. When Jan had asked Hades about it one evening, Hades admitted even he didn't know. Cee didn't know if he believed Hades, since Hades had been around much longer than the brothers had. He had resigned himself to having to trust Hades' word unless proven otherwise. So far, Hades had been truthful about everything Cee had asked him, so he didn't see why he would lie about this.

The bond between each of the Cerberus brothers and their dogs was unique.

"Yes, completely. When we're between dogs, they don't turn to stone when we take the collars off, like Turk did. Can you imagine Diego turning into stone? Well—can you?" Cee was becoming agitated.

Looking down, Theo thought before speaking. "You're right. They haven't turned to stone before."

The connection between the brothers and their companions didn't seem too complicated. They didn't know how it worked, only that it did. Well, up until now.

"I miss Turk. I still can't get over what happened. Is there something I missed that would have saved him?" Cee said to himself while looking back at the statue.

Theo placed his hand on Cee's shoulder. "Honestly, I do not believe you missed anything. If you did, what is done is done, and we can't go back. The Fates have spoken, and we must abide by their word."

"Do you know if Jan has heard anything from Meredith?" Theo asked, trying to get Cee's mind off Turk.

"He said she had called and told him she was still tracking the collar, but she may have to go silent for a bit." Stretching, Cee looked around with fresh eyes. "I think I should go to work, get out of the house. What about having Diego or Sammy go with me?"

At that, Diego perked up and looked excitingly between Theo and Cee.

"Diego said you can take him, and he'll be glad to be away from me. But remember, he likes Blueberry muffins from Bette's place." Theo chuckled at the dog's voice in his head.

3

As Cee drove to Bette's place for Diego's muffin, he thought back to when he first got Turk.

When Honey, Cee's last dog, a golden retriever, started showing signs of slowing down, such as needing a sweater when it got cold or preferring the fireplace to Cee's room, he knew he needed to find a new companion. Searching online he found a local Doberman breeder who was expecting a litter. After ensuring the breeder was legitimate and not a backyard breeder, or worse, something akin to that infuriating wish website, he contacted the breeder to put money down. Since the puppies weren't born yet, he wasn't able to choose a specific puppy and had to wait until he could meet them in person. The litter was born the next day, and Cee took Jan and Theo to meet the new puppies a week later.

All of the puppies except one were snuggled up to their mother, nursing and sleeping on her. The last pup was in the corner looking around, showing an acute sense of place. In fact it seemed to be watching and taking in everything going on around it. Cee knew this was the pup for him and asked if it had already been selected by another buyer. It had not and the breeder marked the pup he chose as sold.

***

By the time the young Doberman was ready to come home, Honey had gotten to the point where she couldn't move without pain.

Cee, the puppy is ready. He is smart and will help you. It is time to let me move on.

"Honey, he just came home. I don't even have a name for him. Please don't go yet, I'm not ready."

This is not the first time you have gotten a new dog. Do you remember when I was a puppy, and you had to let Ruddy go? Honey crawled up to Cee and looked into his eyes. It is time to let the puppy take my spot. I am tired and ready to transition.

"Okay, I will make the appointment with your vet, Dr. Marsh."

Honey was right. She wasn't his first dog. In fact, the brothers had lost count of how many companions they've had over the years. Unlike his brothers, Cee had tried to keep track of past companions. Trying to keep track of historical events and creating lists were part of his personality. When they moved from Greece to Hood River, he had lost the list of companions somewhere. Honestly, it bothered Cee to not remember everything. His brothers acted like it didn't matter, like it was just part of their life and profession. To have companions who help them, but still die far too soon. For all the death he dealt with, you would think the passing of another would just be shrugged off. But for Cee, it always tore at his heart.

On the morning of the appointment, Jan and Theo had asked if Cee wanted them to join him, but he declined the invitation. He needed to do this by himself, and it was easier now that veterinarians existed. In the past, the brothers would have to wait until the companion passed away naturally, as even Theo couldn't bear to hurt a companion. Once Meredith had come into their lives, she would help ease their pain with her knowledge of herbs. He carried Honey to the car and then came back and got the little puppy. It was almost as if the puppy knew what was happening as he climbed into the car and sat next to Honey. When they arrived at the clinic, Cee carried Honey in as the puppy walked next to him, brushing his leg as if in support of what Cee was going through.

As the vet gave Honey the life ending shot, Cee held his breath as Honey took her last. The thought of losing his old friend was heartbreaking. As her heart slowed, Cee spoke to her softly.

"I am going to miss you Honey girl. You were a good dog."

You know I am not leaving forever. I will still be around, just not in this old and broken body.

"I know, but I'll still miss you." Honey gasped one last time before her breathing stopped forever. Cee gingerly removed the collar Honey had worn since she was a pup. The collar was a blue woven material. It was plain, it didn't have sparkles or embroidered words. The two things separating her collar from others was a lack of a leash ring and a large metal clasp which held a red stone. Turning toward the puppy, Cee held out the collar. The Doberman stood stoically while Cee placed it around his neck. With a blink, Cee's head was filled with a surprisingly high-pitched voice.

Hello, are you my new owner?

"No, we are partners. You are my new companion. My name is Cee."

I am Turk. How is it I am able to communicate with you now? We have never been able to communicate in this way before.

"It has to do with the collar. I don't know the specifics, it just is."

Interesting. Are there more of me?

"Well, there are two other dogs who communicate with my brothers, but you can only speak to me. As their companions can only speak to them. You can somewhat speak to the other dogs, but in a different way."

Very interesting indeed. Well, I guess it is time for us to go.

***

Cee stood there for a moment looking at what remained of Honey. Honey had been so intelligent and inquisitive. Each new dog came with a new personality, but Turk's was the closest to his own. It would prove interesting to see how they would get along.

Diego's cold nose on his neck broke Cee out of his memories. Having been brought out of his memories, Cee looked around and realized he had driven all the way downtown and was now in front of Bette's Place. Cee enjoyed the food, but unlike his brother, Theo, he did not eat there regularly.

***

After picking up a blueberry muffin for Diego and a breakfast sandwich for himself, he got back in his BMW and drove out of town. Depending on the day, Cee either worked for Hades at his vineyard or at the gate. Today he was heading out to the gate to take over for Jan, his and Theo's other brother. Since it was just the three of them, they were able to schedule things in a way which worked for all of them without creating too many conflicts.

As he drove up the dirt road, he was considering his choice in vehicles. Even though Theo and Jan constantly gave him crap for driving such a nice car up to the gate, Cee liked his creature comforts. Not only that, but he really liked his 2005 325i. It had the ZHP package which provided specialized modifications which increased the speed, handleability, and comfort of the two door. His car was a bone of contention with his brothers. Most of the time, they all lived and worked well together, but Cee never wanted to go out with them. His brothers sometimes felt he was boring with his nose in a book. It worked to their advantage sometimes, but they would never admit it. This time, it had to do with the fact he wanted a two door versus a four door like they had. It just meant he had to fold the seat down for his companion. At least, with most of the dogs. Turk was an exception to the rule. He rode up front wearing a seatbelt.

***

"You know you can ride in the back, right?"

Yes, but it is not the safest, at least not without a seatbelt. I guess you could reach into the back and place one on me, but I figure it is easier from the front. We wouldn't want an accident to injure us, would we?

While Turk had a point Cee agreed with, it had taken awhile for him to get used to having a large dog sitting upright next to him.

Just thinking about Turk and how he was really just a piece of stone now had Cee hitting the steering wheel with the palm of his hand.

"It just isn't fair. He was such a good dog."

As if Diego knew what he was feeling, Cee felt his cold nose on the back of his arm. It was as if Diego was feeling the same pain.

"It is okay, Diego. Let's get to work and hope Meredith is able to find out who took the stone. Although I don't know what will happen when we get it back. If we get it back, that is."

Cee parked in the small parking lot and opened the door for Diego to jump out of the car. The door appeared to be just part of the rock wall unless you knew what you were looking for. Cee approached the door before placing his hand on a smooth place on the otherwise ordinary stone. A panel of numbers appeared, and Cee entered a four-digit code which caused a click and the door to open.

For someone who works in security, I am still surprised Theo was against this security upgrade.

It had been less than six months since Panterra had returned. A lot had happened since then, including Panterra being kidnapped, Theo killing a God, and another God being killed right after Panterra had visited him. Then Theo and Panterra got married and returned home to Hood River. The day they returned was also the day Turk had turned to stone and Meredith, Jan's wife, had left without a word. What should have been a joyous reunion turned into the start of what has become a nightmare for Cee.

Diego walked in front of Cee as they walked down the hall. Tossing his jacket into the security room, Cee turned toward the door at the far end of the hall.

Get in the game, Cee. You have to be on your game. Especially since we know there is someone behind giving Panterra her freedom. We don't know their endgame, but I don't believe for a minute it was a benevolent action.

Cee straightened up as he walked into the large cavern. To his right was the cascading wall of water, from the outside, created Devil's Punchbowl. To his left was the reason he was living in Hood River with his two brothers, their wives, and their three—no, now two, dogs. The gate to the Underworld.

Standing several stories tall, the stone threshold created the Gate to the Underworld through which all souls would eventually pass. The Gate was the reason Hades had opened a vineyard in Hood River and why the brothers were living here. Cee didn't actually mind living in Hood River. Because he was an academic, where the Gate was located did not matter as much as having a library and access to the internet. He enjoyed not being tied down to one location, other than due to his job.

The gate was made of grayish stone and engraved with runes and words that would flicker on and off depending on the souls who traveled through. Right now, the gate was quiet and dark. *Is Turk's soul out there somewhere?*

Even though Diego had told Cee Turk's soul was still locked in the stone in his collar, he still held out hope his companion's soul had moved on. It would be less painful for both Cee and Turk if it had been released. Souls were strange like that. Even after the eons Cee and his brothers had been in the business of moving them, there were still surprises when it came to souls. This was one of the reasons why the brothers had dogs. The dogs were there not only for companionship but also for security at the gate. The bigger the dog, the better, at least in his mind.

Cee, Jan, and Theo had discussed the scenario on many nights as they struggled with finding a new companion, when their companions had fell ill or were getting older. They had always done so as a group, and they made sure the remaining familiars were in agreeance. It was something they had done for centuries, and it looked like it may have to be done that way again. Cee had once wanted a smaller, dog, like a

Boston Terrier, but it was dismissed by Jan and Theo, mostly Theo.

"Could you imagine how someone would react if they believed Cerberus would be standing majestic and tall at the gates but instead find a tiny, snorting, wheezing Boston Terrier on guard?"

Having a small dog was possible, since the dogs had the ability to create a manifestation of something larger, but without being a large dog, could they really fulfill the role of the illusion?

Over the next four hours, Cee met with two Reapers. One was on the schedule and did not speak during the entire exchange of coins. The other was a special delivery made by one of Panterra's Reapers. He had just reaped an airplane accident. It still felt strange having a reaper boss living in the house, but it was just another day in their crazy lives, Cee thought as he greeted the young reaper.

"Master Cee, how are you?" the reaper asked as he arrived with his bag of coins.

"You do not need to call me Master. Panterra is Master, not I," Cee countered as he began the process of weighing the coins before releasing the souls trapped inside them.

"I respectfully disagree, but I will abide by your wishes and not call you Master again." The reaper turned toward the souls who had been released from the coins. While most of the time the souls were peaceful and would walk to the gate without issues, there was the occasional exception. It was always better for the reaper, and the brother on duty, to be on guard.

Else there could be a chance of someone being hurt or worse.

"Well, I appreciate that. And can you tell the rest of Panterra's Reapers to just call me Cee?"

"Sure. I will send a snap to them once I'm out of the cavern." Nothing electronic or digital worked in the cavern that housed the gate. Cee had tried to get Theo to remedy it, but he kept saying it was something to do with the gate, and there was nothing he could do about it.

"A snap?" Cee looked at the Reaper. What was he talking about?

"Yeah, you know, Snapchat? A social media platform?" The Reaper chuckled. It was amusing at times for the younger Reapers to talk to Cee and Jan, as the brothers were so much older and not technologically advanced at all.

"Oh, I am unsure as to what you're talking about, so it must be a new thing."

"It is a new thing, it's okay. Have Theo tell you about it. He was the one who set it up for us." Theo worked on all sorts of technology for Hades, and as a hobby, so he was always up to date with what was going on.

Just as Cee was about to answer, they heard a scream and looked over to see a man trying to run through the watery portal. He had pushed over a young woman in the process, and it had been her who had screamed. The souls on their way to gate turned back and continued on as if nothing had happened. The reaper walked over and helped the woman up while Diego stood up, stretched, and then loped over to the running soul. As he gained on the man, Diego's body took on the image of a dog three times larger with red eyes.

At the same time, Cee reached under the counter top and picked up his long-handled axe. A robe of black wrapped around him, and his eyes began to emit a crimson glow. Cee was not as tall as Jan at 5'9, but when he was clad all in black, his face obscured by the robe, even he created fear. The robe he conjured had properties which sucked the light from the room. Giving the illusion of a black void moving across the room. The only light was the low, red glow coming from his eyes. Even he looked opposing, a trick he very much needed considering Cee was not known for being a fighter. He advanced on the soul Diego had cornered near the waterfall.

"You can go quietly, or I can cut down your soul right here." Cee's voice was amplified and took on a lower tone when he was wrapped in the shadows. The brothers were not Reapers. They were more often called the boatman when in their work robes, and it is unknown if the brothers were the first to take up the look of the stereotypical reaper or if they adopted it after seeing how the Reapers appear. But either way, it seemed to help with dealing with a troubled soul.

"I'm not ready to leave. I still have stuff to do!" yelled the male spirit.

With more force and emotion than usual, Cee answered, "We don't always get our way. It is time for you to rest, and then you will return when the time is right. Think of it as a nap, or mediation." As he talked, all he could think about was how Turk was gone, possibly forever.

"But...can't I stay a little longer? I have a daughter," said the man, now cowering against the wall as Diego continued to advance. Ready to drag the man through the portal if necessary.

"No. When the Reaper claims your soul, it is time. You can try to fight Fate, but trust me, it is not something you want to do," Cee said, rotating the massive axe in his hands.

"Why?"

"Because Fate is cruel, and she will make it so you never return. And I really do mean never. Your soul will be unable to come back and you will be lost in the mist." Cee was getting frustrated and wanted to be done with this soul.

"How do you know?" asked the man, growing in confidence, as he could hear the anguish in the boat man's voice.

"Because I know Fate. I've met her and even had dinner with her once. She is cold, and cruel." Tired of this conversation and really not wanting to take his chances of possibly calling Fate by using her name so often, Cee stepped forward.

Even though the soul knew it was pointless, he still tried. "No, you have to listen. My daughter, she's a bounty hunter, and she just did her first solo case. She said it was a job bigger than anything even I had done. I really wanted to see her finish it out. The thing is, she's in danger, serious danger. I have to help her."

"Well, if she is in that much danger, I will see her shortly," Cee said coldly while watching Diego move into position to assist in moving the soul along.

Diego leapt forward, grabbing the soul by the leg, and started to drag the man toward the gate. *See a chihuahua couldn't do that*, Cee thought as he ignored the man's cries and pleas.

After watching the giant dog drag the spirit to the gate, the reaper stood for a moment before turning back to Cee. "Mas— I mean Cee, that spirit wasn't on the plane. Oh no, Warden Panterra is going to be so mad. Do you think she will cancel my contract? I just got a new scythe."

"No, she won't, you will be fine. Back to the number of souls, what do you mean he wasn't on the plane?"

"I mean the plane had 100 souls, but when I counted them starting to enter the gate, there was 101, and then this guy took a run for it."

"Well, maybe you miscounted," Cee countered. However, as he looked over the sheet, he realized that the reaper was right. There were only supposed to be 200 coins, two per soul, but the bag weighed as 202 coins, meaning there was an extra soul. Before he could reply, the reaper spoke up with pride.

"Warden Panterra says two of the most important things are to never miscount and to never misplace a coin, and I am sure that I counted correctly," the reaper said.

"Rest easy Reaper, you are correct by my calculations as well. This is strange, but not necessarily something wrong. It has happened before. I mean, things happen. Like the plane could have hit someone, or on your way back a soul slipped in without you knowing."

"You must be right Cee, but it's still strange. I will make sure to let Panterra know." The Reaper took his leave, and Cee returned to the desk. Instinctively, he placed his hand down but instead of the smooth thin head of Turk, his hand rested on the large, rougher block head of Diego. In that moment, Cee remembered Turk was gone. It wasn't only that Turk was gone, it was the way he left, the way he was taken. Anger swelled in Cee's chest. He wasn't ready. With the exception of a couple of wars, all of their dogs had lived lives of normal length. With this, it was as though Turk's life had been snuffed out. Just gone, and even though he wanted to believe Diego that he was still in there, he had to wonder if his friend was gone forever.

And he meant forever. What if they never found the stone, and Cee could never have another partner? Would he be able to guard the gates? Would he ever feel whole again? Cee felt a piece of his being taken away he night Turk had been turned to stone. Some would call it a piece of their heart, but for Cee, it was something more. It was a piece of his soul. Well, if he had a soul. Which, even after being alive for as long as they have been, they were never able to find a definite answer about that one way or the other. Even Hades couldn't, or wouldn't, answer it. And he knew almost everything. Everything except computers, that is. And money. Okay, so there was a lot Hades didn't know, but it was something he should have been able to answer easily. He was the god of the Underworld after all.

For the next six hours, Cee and Diego alternated between the security room and the cavern. They each knew the schedule, and if a reaper did arrive unexpectedly, they could see them outside the waterfall on the camera they had installed. Later that evening, a Reaper appeared near the waterfall. Cee and Diego walked back into the cavern to greet the Reaper and began the process of weighing the coins he had brought.

Cee always wondered about the souls he checked in (or something) and what happened to them once they left the cavern. Much more so than his brothers did. They teased him by saying his studies into soul movement was why he was the 'scholar' versus the other two. He felt it was the fact he wasn't held in a relationship which helped him have the time and mental energy to think about existential subjects.

After the reaper left, Cee began counting all of the coins in the drawer, comparing it to the number that was written in the book. When a Reaper comes in, they give a count of the souls retrieved. Half of the coins go into the drawer, and the other half goes with the soul until they reach the gate, where it disappears. If there is a discrepancy, such as a soul had only one coin, or multiple coins, the Reaper tells the Cerberus brother on duty, and they mark it in the book. As he was finishing, Diego nudged Cee right before Theo burst through the door into the cavern. "Cee, she found it! And apparently, she also found the person who took it." For a moment, Cee was sadly reminded of how it felt to have the type of connection Theo had with Diego before his brain clicked on what Theo had said.

"Wait? Who found what?"

"Meredith found the collar thief, and she called Panterra to help."

"Good. Once we are done, we can throw them through the gates."

"Cee, stop. That's not you talking. You're sounding too much like me, and that's kinda scary. You have to think about this first."

"No Theo, I'm angry. Like, obscenely angry. I will get my revenge," Cee said in a low voice.

"We shall see about that. I know you're angry, but I will not allow you to do something you'll regret." As Theo spoke, his eyes began to burn blue. The blue flames, paired with Theo placing his hand on Cee's shoulder, caused Cee to snap out of his hostile state.

"Then bring them here, and I will yield to you for now," Cee said softening his voice. All the while, Diego was looking back and forth trying his best to follow the conversation.

"We cannot kill them, you hear me? We must find out what is going on before you can get your revenge," Theo added.

"Whatever. Just bring them here." With that, Cee turned away from Theo, effectively ending the conversation.

"I will let Jan know, and we will proceed. It may not be today, as Panterra had to move Reapers around so she could help Meredith. I worry there's more going on here than just someone taking the collar."

"First things first, let's get the collar back and see from there. I need Turk back, Theo," Cee responded as Theo walked out the door.

***

By the next morning, Theo had not returned. Cee figured they had dealt with the thief themselves without Cee being there. It wouldn't surprise him, as he had been overly emotional lately. Being emotional was weird for him, and he didn't understand it himself. In fact, of the three brothers, he was the rock, the one who was never emotional. Now he felt odd, as if he was always on the verge of either crying, killing someone, or both.

With both Theo and Jan absent, Cee manned the gate with Diego. The absence of Turk's voice in his head was a constant reminder of the loss he experienced. Shaking the rapidly returning memories of Turk from his head, he turned back to the work at hand. He continued counting a bag full of coins left by a Reaper who had to hastily dump their coins and leave.

When Cee was preparing to leave another long day of soul counting and Reaper babysitting, he heard a commotion outside the cavern. Diego sat up and stood between Cee and whomever was coming down the hallway. Cee could only see darkness when the door opened. Suddenly the darkness gave way to Sammy, Jan's Boxer companion. Following close behind was Jan and Meredith. Meredith looked at Cee sadly before looking to Jan. As Jan pulled the chain he held forward, a figure stumbled behind them. A slight figure, no more than 5'6" tall, wearing a leather duster two sizes too big with their pale hands chained together. Cee couldn't see their face as the duster's hood obscured any features. Panterra could be seen slightly prodding them with the handle of her scythe while Theo walked behind the group, keeping watch. Cee wanted to rush forward, but Diego stood between him and the group, holding him back from joining his brothers.

The search party walked in front of the desk, further keeping Cee from them. He noticed Diego had stopped paying attention to him, allowing for Cee to creep around the desk. All of a sudden, Cee's eyes lit red, and his body grew several inches taller. A black robe cast all but his glowing eyes in shadows. Transformed, Cee pushed the stranger against the cavern wall with his hand on their throat. Cee expected the throat of a man. However, as he continued to push, he realized it was thinner, possibly that of a woman. He felt his brother's hands on him, but he only saw red.

"Cee, STOP! You must stop. We need answers. We can't get answers if they're dead." The words barely broke through his anger. He didn't know who said it, but it didn't matter who it was. His vision clouded by the desire for revenge. As Cee was just about to crush his vengeance into the trembling figure, he realized the man who had caused so much pain and turmoil for him was no man at all. It was a woman. *A woman stole the collar?* Cee thought as he loosened the hand on her throat. Taking a quick look around, he did not immediately seethe collar. "Where is the collar?" As he saw everyone look away or shake their head, he knew his revenge would have to wait. There would be time for it, but not now, and not here.

As Cee removed his hand from her throat, the hood of her duster fell back, and revealed a bright red braid circling a pale face full of freckles. Looking at him over tearstained green eyes was a young woman. Upon seeing her fully, Cee immediately took a step back. Meredith glared at Cee's brash behavior before she stepped closer to help Panterra. Both held the woman up as she coughed and gasped for air.

"Who...Who are you? Why did you take the collar?" Cee stammered, shocked by her beauty but still outraged by the fact she had taken his companion away. There was also something familiar about her. Something made him think they had met before.

The cavern was silent for only about 15 seconds, but to Cee, it felt like an eternity. The woman finally caught her breath and began to speak.

"My name is Brandy, who are you guys, and why am I here?"

"You are here because you stole something of mine," Cee replied, with less emotion in his voice than before.

"I didn't steal anything from anyone. Why would I steal from you anyway? Are you going to kill me?

Panterra placed her hand on Brandy's shoulder. "No one is going to kill you."

"Tell that to that monster there." Brandy glared at Cee.

"On my life, he will not touch you again. At least for now," Jan replied as he stepped up next to Meredith. Theo and the dogs held back in the event Brandy decided to run.

Raising her chin in defiance Brandy replied, "Oh, that really makes me want to talk. What should we talk about? The weather? Where I am? Hey, should I get a lawyer?"

"I don't think tha—"

Cee cut off his brother's comment for the time being. "Have we met before?"

Brandy briefly looked over Cee. "Not that I remember. But then again, you aren't very memorable. I would, however, remember your eagerness to kill a lady, you monster."

"You are not a lady," Cee quipped back.

Jan stepped back in, pushing Cee aside. "Do you know who we are? You should, so either you are lying or are just plain stupid."

"Consider, well, let's see. To start with, this green lady has been following me for who knows how long. Which, by the way, I think there is something seriously wrong with you. You may want to see a doctor or something, because that's definitely not normal," she said addressing Merideth. "Then, I get kidnapped from my home by this goth chick I've never seen before." Looking at Panterra who did a small wave back. "Now, I'm in a cavern with three strange guys, one who just tried to kill me. Oh, and two dogs who look like they want to eat me. Is that close enough for you? Or should we sit around and drink tea as we discuss who you are?" The woman was becoming more confidant with each word she spoke.

Cee felt a bit of admiration for Brandy. She must know her life was in danger, but she was putting on a rather strong front.

"Well, let me explain what you did and where you are. You broke into our house. You then stole a collar off of a dog, which if you haven't realized yet, was not just some trinket bought at the pet store. You then ran when Meredith," Jan pointed to his wife, "who you so aptly called the 'Green lady', tried to stop you. How am I doing good so far?"

Brandy nodded.

"Then, when Panterra here," Jan pointing to Panterra, "who you called the "goth chick", tried to talk to you, you tried to kill her. Which, if you knew who she was would be laughable, but for now, let's assume you don't. So, she approached you about the collar. However, you got brazen, and she doesn't take kindly to brazen." With that comment, Theo nudged Panterra with his elbow. She looked at him as she rolled her eyes.

While Cee wanted to comment, he knew Jan had a plan. He couldn't trust his own emotions to be clear headed enough at this moment to get the answers they all needed before he killed her. Part of his brain was asking if he could kill her now. She may not have known what she was doing. However, the emotional side still mourning for Turk refused to even consider what the logical part was saying.

Focusing on Jan's conversation with Brandy, Cee realized he was starting to ask questions and would demand answers.

"So, now that we are up to date, I have some questions for you. I guess you don't have to answer, but you should if you knew what was good for you. I mean, we could always just get our boss to handle you. I'm sure you have heard of him. Hades, the God of the Underworld? Does that name ring a bell?"

With that, Brandy's eyes went large and she took four steps backwards before she felt the wall behind her.

"I didn't know who you are talking about. What is going on? Where are we?" With that, Brandy broke down in tears. Cee didn't believe her theatrics for one minute and as he looked around, he could see no one else was believing it either. Feeling more in control of his emotions, he chided himself internally.

"We don't buy it. You know who we are, or you at least have some idea of what is going on."

Standing tall again, Brandy wiped the fake tears away. "Yes, I know you are the Cerberus, and I accepted a bounty for one of the heads." Cee heard Jan and Theo chuckle while Panterra gasped.

"Did you really think you could kill one of us? One of the Cerberus? How? By taking the collar?"

Looking proud of herself, Brandy replied, "I liked the way it looked. However, the bounty was for Janus Cerberus, not you." Brandy tossed her head toward Jan and then glared at Cee.

"Wait, are you talking about the bounty hanging in Ireland?" Theo suddenly asked.

"Yes, why?" Brandy looked slightly worried, but still stood tall.

"Didn't you wonder why the paper was so old? Why it was hard to read? Why there were only two bounties on that entire wall?" Theo continued while looking her over. Cee cocked his head at Theo's intent interrogation of Brandy, but focused on her answer.

"My da said I could finally have my own bounty. He and my brothers have been hunters for as long as I can remember, and while I went with them sometimes, I never got to solo before."

A small bell rang in Cee's ears, but he couldn't place the memory it invoked.

A red headed man with slumped shoulders trying to convince someone of something. "No, it is okay. My daughter is a bounty hunter."

In the heat of the moment, Cee couldn't figure out why the memory was important. Putting it to the back of his mind, he again focused on the present.

"So, you just walked up to the bounty board and decided you would take the oldest one there? Seriously?" Jan continued the interrogation.

"I had to prove myself. Do you know how hard it is to be a female bounty hunter? In my family, I am the first. I took what looked to be hard, but not impossible."

Cee respected her spirit and he felt a curiosity towards he spunky bounty hunter.

"Okay, but why did you take the collar?" Cee asked.

"Well, I thought if I took the collar, it might be worth something to you all with that stone, and I could lead you into a trap. However, with the green lady following me, I seemed to be the one to fall into a trap myself."

Jan chuckled again at the Green lady comment, while Meredith lightly slapped his arm.

"Wait, you can see she's green? Like how green?" Cee asked. Meredith was green. Being a dryad, her hair and skin were both shades of green. Though, to normal humans, she only appeared sun kissed, not actually green.

"Well her hair is green, and her skin is a darker green. Can't you all see that?"

"Yes, we can see that, but you shouldn't be able to." Jan looked closer at her, as if he was trying to see inside her.

"Dude back off, you're creeping me out."

Jan took a step back, unsatisfied. "Back to the questions at hand. Where is the collar?"

"In a safety deposit box at an undisclosed location," Brandy replied, her smug tone coming through perfectly.

As his eyes burned red with his rekindled fury, Cee got into her face. "You will get it. I will be coming with you."

For the first time, Brandy lost her composure. She could feel the hate rolling off the shorter man.

Jan stepped forward and placed his hand on Cee's shoulder. "You are not going anywhere with someone who wants to kill us. We can't close you."

"Yes, I will. Turk was my dog, but the bounty wasn't for me. Isn't that right Brandy?" Her name left a foul taste in his mouth.

"Um, maybe we should get Hades involved? Just so, you know. Just in case," Theo tried to interject.

"No, this was my Turk. I need to see it through."

Cee turned away from the woman and stalked from the room, his face still hot with anger.

5

"I still don't think it is a good idea, Cee. You don't know who's helping her." Jan tried to make his brother see his point of view.

Cee was not listening as he continued to throw clothes into a backpack. "Like I said, I have to do this myself."

"Well, Panterra is going to be shadowing you. If not her, at least some of her Reapers. Before you say anything, this will happen, so you can either agree to it, or not. I am past the point of arguing."

Cee knew his brothers had his health and wellbeing in mind and knew there was no point in fighting. Long ago, Cee had realized the was not a fighter, unlike his brothers.

"Okay, whatever you think is best." With that, both Theo and Jan looked at each other, surprised Cee had given in already but knowing better than to question it. Jan folded a shirt before handing it to him. "We will be here watching over the Gate. Go get the collar and we can handle everything here. Oh, and try not to kill her. Killing isn't really your thing."

"I am not going to kill her as long as she still has the collar or knows where it is."

The brothers walked from the room. "Jan, I don't think he could kill her even if he wanted to. Panterra said she put up one hell of a fight." The rest of the conversation faded into the distance, but Cee wasn't listening as he continued to pack.

***

"Are you ready?" Cee asked Brandy was as she stood tall and beautiful by the waterfall. Her red hair was loose and blowing slightly in the breeze. Even the freckles splashed across her delicate nose seemed to come alive. Cee shook his head. Remember, she is the enemy.

"Whatever gets me away from you and your bunch of weirdos and back to my family."

"Well then, hold my hand, and we will go to Dublin."

"Umm... Why do I need to hold your hand? Why wouldn't we just jump on a plane or something?" Brandy looked around, confused by his statement.

37

"Ahh, no. We are flying Cerberus style." With that, Cee grabbed her hand and thought of Dublin.

A portal opened and Brandy could barely make out what she thought was the Wicklow Mountains near Dublin. Brandy was reluctant at first, but eventually Cee pulled her forward. She closed her eyes, hoping both her body and the mountains she saw were in fact in Ireland. She didn't know what they had gone through, but she didn't want to get stuck somewhere.

As they strode toward a field full of sheep, Cee looked over at Brandy. "You can open your eyes. We're here." Brandy opened one eye and looked around nervously before opening the other one. When she realized she was on solid ground, she dropped Cee's hand and turned toward him. "What the hell did you do?"

"I thought you knew everything and had all the answers? That was a portal we walked through. It's a doorway connecting two locations. Anyone can do it but most people don't have the concentration to pull it off.

Brandy completely ignored the question and contemplated what he had said.

"Hey Brandy, where to?" Cee said softly, she responded by pointing toward the center of town.

As they walked, Cee looked toward her. "Do you have any idea who we are or what you have gotten yourself into?" Cee asked breaking the silence.

She knew little about the brothers other than what the bounty on the wall had said. It was a simple 'Janus Cerberus wanted for high crimes against the Gods. Wanted dead. Be careful of the dog'. The line about the dog had confused her until she arrived and saw Turk. Figuring they only had one dog, not three. Brandy had thought taking the collar would show her ability, and maybe the stone would be worth something to the brothers, especially if it lured Jan out to where she could kill him. The minute Meredith had begun to track her she realized that she was in over her head. There was no way in hell she was going to admit it to this ruggedly handsome man, whom she was seeing in a different light now that he was not so emotional. She had never like overly emotional men. She was far from stupid, and her father and brothers had always told her to listen more and talk less because you never know what secrets people are willing to spill in a moment of weakness.

Cee let Brandy lead while keeping a close eye on her and where she was taking them. Instead of going through the newer parts of town, she led them through back alleys with stone paths. The houses in this part of town were falling down, with missing roofs and collapsed stone walls. This part of town was left to the ravages of time. Cee shook his head at the waste of history all around him. Cee watched her as they side stepped stones, wondering how much he should tell her. She was a bounty hunter. Her sole missions were to steal, kill, and otherwise engage in illicit activity. Cee did not have a very high regard for bounty hunters even before this most current encounter.

As they walked, Cee remembered what his brother had said about him being a killer. Even though he had never taken a life, many had considered him one just because he was aa Cerberus. He was the thinker, the one who took everything in, while Jan was the leader, able to command an army if needed. It had been that way since they were younger. The fact he was even considering killing someone bothered and confused him. He had seen lives ended plenty of times. He was a Cerberus after all, but never had the blood been directly on his hands. Even during the dryad wars, he was always in the background. He was more of a planner and organizer than a fighter. Thinking about it now, he wondered how many had died due to his battle plans. How much blood had been spilled by his words? That blood was on his hands as well, even if he never performed the final blow.

What confused Cee was the fact he didn't hate Brandy. He was upset and wanted to find the collar, but he no longer wanted her death. There was another feeling there, something he had felt only once before. Before he could get too far down that rabbit hole, Brandy cleared her throat.

"Uh, Earth to Cee. You coming, or are you just planning to stand there looking like an idiot?"

Cee tossed her an annoying glance.

With a 'humph', Brandy flipped her braid off her shoulder and cut through a grass field on her way to another stone road. "Well, since you decided to drop us nowhere near my home, we have some distance to cover in order to get your precious collar back."

"It isn't the collar. Well, not completely. It's mainly the stone," Cee replied following her. He couldn't help but notice how the leather duster swayed with Brandy's hips as she walked. She must be doing that on purpose, he thought.

Brandy was intentionally swaying her hips with each step. If she was stuck with this stick in the mud guy, she may as well as have some fun with it. Soon she would be able to alert her brothers and father to what was happening. They would surely kill him. Heck, a little fun with him before he died may help cast away the feeling of dread she's had since she took the collar. When she had walked up to the large Doberman, he had just stood there. He didn't bark, he didn't try to bite her, nothing. He just stood there. Like he was waiting for her. Even when she had taken the collar off, he hadn't moved more than blinking his eyes at her. The hair on the back of her neck had tingled, and she'd felt a zap of power as she pulled it free. It was something that had only happened to her a couple of times before, but never in this type of situation. Before taking on this solo bounty, she had only gone on hunts with her family. She had been primarily tasked with finding objects for clients. It definitely wasn't as glorious as hunting down criminals, but it paid the bills.

"What's the deal with the collar? Is it, like, old or something? Why can't you just get another one? I understand family heirlooms and stuff, but you seem really angry about the old fabric strap."

"You could say that. It has been part of my family for as long as I can remember." He left out the fact that his memory spanned thousands of years. He also wasn't quite sure how old the collar was. The three collars with stones had shown up when the brothers were living in Greece. He vaguely remembered instructions, but not what they were. To this day, Theo still talks about how much he hates that they don't live in Greece anymore. They had all become accustomed to the people and the land. Cee hated change as it messed with his process. He was logical and analytical and liked things a certain way. That is why he tended to not leave the house unless it was for work or infrequently to go out with his brothers. Yes, Oregon was colder, but Hades seemed happy, and if the boss man was happy, then Cee was as well.

"Ahh, so it is a family heirloom. I have a bunch of those. Well, my da said they were from my mom's side of the family, but I don't know much about her. All I know is that I look like her, and they weren't bounty hunters. That's all my Da's side."

Cee looked at Brandy. "I didn't know my parents. Or at least, I don't really remember them. It has only ever been me and my brothers, Jan, and Theo. Well, and our dogs." He cringed as he remembered Turk.

It went quiet for a bit while both Cee and Brandy digested the information they each just learned from the other.

"So, I need to know, why did you all spend so much effort to track me down to recover a collar? Like really, it's just a collar."

Cee thought on this for a moment, and his willingness to talk got the better of him. "It's not just any collar. The stone is like a conduit, or so it seems to be. When our pets have the stone around their necks, we can communicate with them."

She started laughing. "You really want me to believe you can talk with dogs?" She quit when she realized he was not kidding.

"Wait, you mean you can actually communicate with animals?" While not believing Cee, she decided to play along for a bit. "Are they smart? Like you know, do they understand what's going on?" she asked.

"Yes. They are incredibly smart, and Turk, my dog who you killed, was amazing." She stepped back shocked, now realizing why he was mad.

"Wait. What? No. I didn't kill your dog. I just took the collar, and he even let me have it," Brandy said, putting her hands up trying to shield herself from the thought.

Cee sat down on a large bolder off the side of the road and hunched over. "Yes. By removing the collar, you killed Turk. I don't know how or why, but it does not change that it happened."

Brandy put her face in her hands. "I am so sorry. I never would have taken it if I had known." Tears slid down her cheeks. She turned to hide the weakness from Cee, but he had already noticed.

"How much further do we have? I need to get back." In reality, Cee wanted to get the collar back onto Turk's neck, knowing it would bring him back to life.

She regained her composure and answered him, "Once we get to Dublin, I need to leave you for a bit while I get it."

He laughed at her absurdity. "Absolutely not. I don't know my way around Dublin. I'm not letting you out of my sight. At least, not until I have the collar in my hand. I don't care about your hiding place. I need that collar, and I don't trust you."

Brandy weighed her options. She could double back and alert her brothers and father. She didn't know if she should trust him with her family's secrets. While she didn't believe Cee didn't know his way around Dublin, she did believe he didn't care. She didn't understand why it hurt to think that he didn't care about her, but it did. Shaking her head, she remembered what her Da had told her and her brothers numerous times as they grew up, *Don't trust anyone other than family. They will stab you in the back as easy as they smile to your face.* To date, it had served her well to not trust people, but it also made for a lonely life.

"Look, I don't care if you trust me or not, but I need that collar. Then you can go about your bounty hunter life, and leave me and mine alone."

"Cee, I took Jan's bounty. My reputation depends on its completion."

"Can't you just rehang the poster and walk away? No one will ever have to know," Cee countered.

"Yes and no. I could hang the poster back, but what kind of hunter would I be?"

"Well, a living one to start with. Think about it– You were tracked down by the wives of my brothers. Who...well let's just say they just don't have the same kind of special skills my brother, Theo, has. Well I guess technically Panterra, the one you called the 'goth chick' is pretty powerful, and I'm not quite sure exactly how much power Meredith–oh I am sorry the 'green lady' as you so aptly called her– has. I digress though, back to Theo. Have you ever heard of the Blue Tide in battles?"

She thought for a second. "Yeah. The saying goes something like 'A single individual can turn the tide of battle, and the wave will crush the enemy'."

"Well close, but that saying, or legend, is actually about my brother. He IS the blue tide. How does the owner of the bounty know it was you who took the job? Have you spoken to them?" Cee asked, changing the subject.

Brandy cocked her head at Cee. "Well of course, how else do you think I found out where you live, and how do you think I found out that if I took the collar you would come looking for me?"

"But why take Turks collar if you were after Jan and not me?" Cee asked.

"I don't really know. That's just what the man in the shadows told me. 'now take the red stone and collar.' I figured it would draw Jan out. I didn't know there were multiple dogs." She raised her voice at the end, expressing her frustration at being interrogated. "The bounty had been there for a long time, and no one else wanted it. They obviously knew something I didn't..." With that statement, Brandy fell silent.

Now intrigued, Cee kept pushing. "What?"

"I was just thinking about the bounty and why my Da or brothers never took it. I mean why didn't they take it themselves or at least warn me?" she said, talking to herself.

"Maybe because they knew it was a lost cause. Like I said earlier, there is much more to the Cerberus brothers than you know. Honestly, any bounty hunter who would have taken the bounty would likely not have lived long enough to talk about why they shouldn't have. Any experienced bounty hunter would have already heard the stories and known that." On the edge of Cee's memory came a flash of a soul he had recently met, also red-haired, and talking about his daughter. There was something he was trying to remember, but it just wouldn't connect.

Cee again considered how much to tell her. Brandy was human with a normal life span. Nothing she could say would really affect Cee or his brothers, but he was still cautious. Cee had seen enough in his long life to know that trouble came in threes, and so far there had already been two. First Panterra had come back into their lives with the assignment to reap Theo. Then Turk turned into stone.

"You mean no other hunter has ever came after your brother before now?" she questioned.

"Let's just say that in the past, when people went up against us, they ended up no longer one of the living." There was no need to mention it was Theo who usually protected the family in that respect. He remembered the time when random masked guys had approached them when the three had been travelling through China right after the Gate had moved to Hood River. But they changed their mind after half of them lay dead on the ground.

Before Brandy could respond, Cee called out, "Looks like we are getting close to the city. I can see buildings."

Breathing a sigh relief at almost being home, Brandy pushed back her questions and hoped getting rid of Cee would stop the fuzzy feeling she had in her stomach.

"Continue leading the way, oh great Bounty Hunter," Cee joked. He was actually enjoying her company, which was starting to outweigh his feelings of dread when he looked at her. While he was still worried about Turk, he was starting to enjoy spending time with Brandy. She was beautiful, snarky, and had an internal strength about her he wasn't convinced she knew she had.

He was surprised neither Meredith nor Panterra, two women who should have been able to sense it, didn't say anything. Maybe they had been as preoccupied as he was. He would have to ask them when he returned home.

Brandy led Cee through twists and turns of town until they crossed over the Royal Canal and reached the inner city. Cee hadn't bothered to keep track of where they were. He didn't have any need to return to where they had been.

Suddenly, Brandy stopped. Cee not completely paying attention, ran into her back. Stepping back, he looked around before catching her waist to stop her from falling.

"What's wrong?" Cee breathed into her ear. Bad decision, Cee reprimanded himself as he soaked in the clove scent of her hair.

"I don't know, but something feels off. Like something is missing."

Cee shook his head. "Wait, like what is missing? It had better not be my collar." His voice filled with urgency.

"I don't know, something just feels wrong." With that, Brandy turned the corner into a dead-end alley. Walking toward the red brick wall, she looked around before placing her hand on the wall. With a slight push, a section of the wall began to ease open.

"Impressive work. Is this your creation?" Cee admired the wall as they walked through it. There really was nothing to distinguish the door from the surrounding wall. Being that it was midday and the sun was shining from directly above, Cee felt as though he should have been able to see something to set it apart. *I need tell Theo and Jan about this; it may help us with the door leading to the gate.*

"Where is everything?" Brandy yelled as she walked deeper into the room.

Everything is still here, or Brandy has a bit of a hoarding issue. Cee thought as he took in the entire space. How she was able to discern if something was missing was beyond him. The space screamed of an open concept, except for the mounds of junk creating partitions. By looking around at the walls and structural support, it seemed like this room was much older than Brandy, and maybe even himself. Every available space was full of objects spanning centuries and locations. As he walked past an Egyptian canopic jar, he ran his hand over the jackal shaped lid. When his fingers touched the top, a tendril of power reached out to him. *Something for later. Collar first, weird Egyptian jar later.*

"What's missing? I see lots of stuff. Actually, there are things here I think might belong to me," he said upon seeing a tapestry of a fallen angel in the corner.

"The money and the notes. They're gone." Brandy was frantically searching a pile of papers on an ancient high-backed wooden chair.

"Is the collar here?" Cee asked.

"Don't rush me, this is important. More important than you can probably grasp," she said while continuing to frantically search the pile.

"Slow down, bounty hunter. Explain to me what's going on and I may be able to help. I am pretty smart after all." Cee hadn't necessarily meant to offer his assistance, but he was beginning to like Brandy. Even if she was his nemesis.

"Wait, you said some of this was yours. How old are you? You look like you're 25, and most of these items are centuries old." Brandy's voice was muffled as she continued to rifle through stuff.

Considering his response, he went with the tried and true answer. "Thank you, but I have actually lived in Hood River since before Hood River was even a town. I was there before Lewis and Clark traveled the Columbia River. Before that, I lived in Greece."

"Interesting. I never kept up with United States history. What is that, like 40 years?"

"Sure, let's go with that," he said, shaking his head. "Can I help you?"

"Thank you for asking, but you don't know what I'm looking for," she said as she moved her search to another pile.

No, but I do know exactly what I'm looking for.

"Okay, well, I'll just sit in that chair over there." Cee began to tiptoe through stuff on his way to the high-back chair made from what appeared to be redwood and velvet.

"Yeah, that's fine. Just be careful. I've heard it bites."

Cee looked at the chair and touched the armrest. The chair looked like a chair Cee had seen before, but there was no way it was the same one. Nudging the chair's leg with his toe, Cee looked around for another place to sit. Finding another chair that did not look like it was going to chew on him, he sat down. It was much more comfortable than he expected, but he wasn't going to just sit there looking like an idiot while the leather duster flitted here and there searching for his stuff.

"Not to rush you, but can we get the collar?"

"No, this is my family's bounty trove. We store everything here that we have either acquired in the process of jobs, or things that were never paid for by clients. It has been in the family for generations. Da says it's been here since before Dublin was here. When I got old enough to start working with my family, I realized I needed my own space. It wasn't that I didn't trust my family, but some of the things I tracked down did weird things."

Following Brandy toward the back, Cee couldn't help himself. Always interested in learning more, he had to ask, "What type of weird things?"

"You would think me crazy," she said, looking at Cee.

"You would be surprised by what I'm willing to believe," Cee said, still surprised she thought him a simpleton.

Brandy looked him over. *Yes, yes maybe so. I wonder what's under that sweater.* Shaking her head to get the image of a shirtless Cee out of her mind, she went back to the task at hand. A small stone door, no more than 5 feet tall, was nestled into the back wall. "I found this cavern when I was young and playing around in here when I wasn't supposed to be. My Da was always so busy I doubt he even knew I found it. It seemed to call to me, and I went to it. It opened up, and when Da wasn't looking, I climbed in. He didn't realize I was gone until the stone had closed behind me. He said he called for me until his voice was hoarse, but I never once heard him. I did hear a female voice telling me it was time to go, so I came back into this room and watched him hysterically throwing things, like I was playing hide and go seek or something. I never did tell him about the room because it was mine, you know?" Chuckling, Brandy closed her eyes. "*Oscail*," she spoke quietly, and the door slide up.

Knowing Gaelic when he heard it, Cee asked, "Did you just ask it to open?"

She ignored his question. "After that first time, I would come here every chance I got. Many times after, the door wouldn't open. I tried everything I could think of. It was my secret and I needed it. I needed that space. Growing up in a house of all boys and no mom, I needed something just for me." Brandy stepped through the doorway, ducking her head slightly.

When Cee didn't move, Brandy looked back. "Aren't you coming?"

"I didn't know if I was allowed," Cee answered.

"Of course you are. Now let me find the collar. Don't be scared," she said tongue in cheek.

Cee gingerly stepped over the threshold into what he thought would be a smaller space. It was, however, much bigger than he thought it would be. When he placed his hands on the inner wall, he could feel the magic flowing and wondered how a young souled human bounty hunter came into possession of such a strong magical cavern like this. He had heard from Meredith that these types of things occasionally sprung up, but they were not common and were rarely accessible by the unaware. *Maybe Brandy isn't as human as she looks,* Cee thought.

"Well that's strange."

Rolling his eyes, Cee suspected nothing good could come from Brandy saying that.

"Did you just roll your eyes at me?" Brandy stood up with her hand on her hip.

"Yes, I did. Everything that has been happening is a bit strange, so what is 'strange' this time?"

"Well, my life is usually pretty normal. However, this is not. Normally things stay where they are supposed to, and things have randomly appeared out of nowhere in a long time."

"What did you mean about things 'staying where they are supposed to' and what just appeared?" Cee wanted to get home, but he was also drawn to Brandy.

"Well, the collar was in one place when I left. But when we got here, it was in a different place right next to this painting." Brandy held up a large painting of a human with canine features. He was standing in front of a forge, holding a great hammer in one hand and what appeared to be a red gem in the other.

Cee ignored the painting as he looked for the collar in her hands. "Can I have it please?"

A flash of red flew at Cee, his reaction time just fast enough to grab the object before it hit him in the face. Looking it over, he ran his fingers over the stone and the worn fabric. Raising it to his face, Cee closed his eyes and breathed in the memory of not only Turk, but of all the other companions he had shared time with as well.

Brandy continue looking at him, questioning if he knew the painting, especially since the collar was near it.

Initially, Cee figured he would not know who was depicted in the painting. However, memories began to flood back as he looked at it. Cee had always liked art. As a matter of fact, he remembered that very painting hanging in his old house south of London. "That is Fenrir. He was sort of a demi-wolf god who was the son of Loki and some giant, but her name escapes me now." He couldn't help but wonder how the painting ended up here.

"Was?" she asked, cocking her head to the side much like a dog does when they are trying to understand what you are saying.

"Yeah, the story goes he got too powerful or upset a powerful person." Cee shook his head trying to separate the truth from the lore. "Fenrir was captured and then thrown into the Furnace with the Titans. He either couldn't be held, or Reapers let him out. Either way, he was released and went on a rampage. After killing a lot of other souls, he was finally killed by Víðarr, son of Odin."

"What's the furnace?" she asked.

"Oh, well that is a long story. Ask Panterra if you ever run into her again."

"Was she the goth one?" she asked, dropping the painting lower.

Cee nodded in response.

Brandy looked between the painting and the collar Cee was holding next to his chest. "You don't see it, do you?"

"See what?" Cee asked as he turned to leave.

"The gem in your collar looks like the same gem he's holding in this painting," Brandy said as if she were talking to a child.

Cee turned and looked at the painting. "I don't think so. It looks a bit familiar, but I can't place if I have seen it before. Anyway, how did you come by that painting?"

"What in Odin's name are you talking about? You are so fucking dense. This painting has been here since I was a kid. It showed up right after I started coming here more frequently. As for your precious collar, it was over here in this box. It gave me a jolt when I grabbed it, so you should be careful." She calmed her tone and continued, "I'm sorry that my taking that old-ass collar caused you to lose your dog. I was always more of a cat person, but I still would not have wished that on anyone. I don't see how I hurt the dog. I just took off its collar. I didn't hurt it at all." With her rant over, Brandy took a deep breath.

"Slow down. Even I'll admit this is strange, alright?" Cee tried to play dumb, but he knew something else was going on. He needed to get back to Oregon and find out what that something was. He had felt the magic of the room, which meant either Brandy had magic and had been leading him on, or she was truly oblivious. *Guess there is only one way to find out.*

"Do you feel this room?" he asked.

"What do you mean by feel this room?" She looked even more puzzled.

"The magic? The power? The security it gives you?" he said, drawing on his personal beliefs.

"What? No. I mean, it's always just felt safe. Wait, do you mean magic? Magic isn't real," she said forgetting they had walked across the world in seconds.

Yup, just apparently oblivious.

"Yes, it is. You can feel magic when you are around it enough. The main room of your 'bounty trove' is normal, but this room? This room has magic flowing through it. Quite a bit actually. That's why I asked to come in."

"You didn't ask me if you could come in. Oh wait, you did."

"An Individual's magical place is theirs to command and control. I could not enter without your permission. Unlike what you did at my house," his voice dripping with sarcasm.

She shrugged it off and subtly reached for something behind her.

"You don't have to worry about me. I know I said I was going to kill you in the end, but that feeling has passed. You can put the dagger down, Brandy."

Before Brandy could respond, a scuffling sound came from the main room, not unlike a group of mice moving through dried brush.

Cee turned toward the sound.

"Don't worry, it's just my brothers or my Da. Stay behind me and they won't see you." Brandy began to walk toward the door when Cee put his arm out.

Mouthing to her "be quiet," Cee stepped forward and sniffed.

Making a face and trying to get around him, Brandy pushed forward.

Cee turned his head slightly and glared. "NO," he hissed and pushed her back into the room.

With that, he stepped silently into the room. After about 30 seconds, he rushed back into the room. "Tell the room to close the door, NOW!" he whispered to Brandy.

"What? Why?"

"Please just do it. I will explain when we are safe."

Brandy closed her eyes and spoke softly, "*dluth*." The door began to slide down quickly but silently. When it finally clicked into place, Cee let out the breath he hadn't realized he had been holding.

"Those weren't your family. Unless they are shapeshifting guards from the Underworld," the words rushed out of him.

Fearfully, Brandy started looking around. "How do they know about this place? Can they get in here? What is going on? Where is my family? This place is supposed to be secure. How are we supposed to get out?" She shot off questions faster than Cee could track them. He was surprised when she slumped in his arms.

Not realizing what he was doing until Brandy was in his arms, Cee placed a hand on the back of her head. "I don't know. I don't have the answers to your questions. I do know they cannot hear us in here due to the magic. I don't know about your family, but we have to get back to mine. My brothers may have some answers as to what is going on. It appears we were not the only ones after you." Almost forgetting the reason he had come all the way to Dublin, Cee saw the collar in the hand he had wrapped behind Brandy's back.

"No!" she said, pulling away quickly, ashamed of showing weakness. "I am not going anywhere. I have a family to protect, and in the event of a breach, we are to meet at the house," she said, gathering herself up.

Admiring her spunk and resolve, Cee weighed his options. "No, first we get out of here. Then we will return for your family with help."

Brandy wanted to fight, but he was right. If there was someone looking for her and wanting to hurt her, then they may also be after her Da and brothers, and her main concern was for them. It had been just the four of them her entire life, and she couldn't imagine it without them.

"Grab anything you think you will need, and I will get us out of here. Make it quick though. Make sure to also grab that painting and the dagger." Cee pressed his ear to the door. He couldn't hear anything, but he could feel they were still out there.

"Okay, I think I got everything I need."

"That was quick. How did you even pack everything you may need? I don't know if you'll be able to come back." Cee had turned toward Brandy to help her when he noticed not only did she have the painting, but had also found a backpack that looked to be bursting at the seams. "Wait? Where did you get the backpack?"

"I don't know, I've never seen it before. When I went for the dagger, the backpack was there. What's strange is that it was already full of things I hadn't thought about grabbing. It was like it knew I would need them. I don't ask questions in here," she said with a shrug of her shoulders.

It is time to go my dear. I will see you again. Trust the brothers as they will never lead you astray.

"Did you hear that?" Brandy looked around.

"Hear what?" Cee looked up from the painting.

"I just heard a voice. You didn't hear it?" she said, still looking for the source.

"Nope, are you ready to go?" Cee was too preoccupied to try and solve the problems in Brandy's head.

Looking around once more to see if she had everything, she grabbed Cee's hand and nodded.

Cee concentrated on his house. He thought of the roof, the walls, and the way the paint was peeling on the second story. In front of them, a window into Cee thoughts opened, showing a house with a green lawn. Cee looked back at the stone door, worrying why the guards were in Dublin. He didn't stay around to see whose rune they wore on their chest plate. If he knew their master, it might shed some light on these dark times. But to really see the runes it would take an up-close encounter, and the Cerberus didn't necessarily get along with the guards. Guards didn't usually go far from their charge, and so there was a chance Cee could come face to face with God. Even worse if it was one of those egotistical Gods who thought they were better than the others. Sadly, that consisted of most of them.

Thankfully, Jan and Theo dealt with them most of the time. Especially Theo, but his dealing with them usually ended in blood. Like recently when he took out one of the top reaper leaders. When Theo went on his rampage, Cee thought him reckless, risking his life and the Underworld for a woman. But right now, he was willing to risk his life for Brandy. At least with Theo, he and Panterra had a very long, yet complicated, history. Brandy stole from them. Ugh, he should just leave her to her own fate. But he couldn't do it. Turk would know what to do in this situation. Actually, he probably wouldn't. Honey would have though. She had way more heart than logic. Turk was all logic. Turk would have had him leave her.

In a blink, Cee and Brandy were standing in front of a large, light-colored house. In the driveway were Cee's BMW and Theo's Land Rover. "Welcome to my home," Cee said, reluctantly letting go of Brandy's hand to open the door.

"Cee, remember I've been here before. However, under different circumstances."

"Yeah, I remember," Cee snorted.

Before Brandy could respond, they stepped into the living room to the welcoming sounds of Diego barking. Cee placed the painting down near Turk and motioned for the backpack from Brandy.

She handed it over and took to looking around the living room. Their house wasn't huge, but it was big enough for what they needed. The living room, dining room, and kitchen were mostly open with a bar separating the kitchen from the dining room, and there were several doors leading out to individual rooms.

Diego ran up, sniffed Cee, and then walked over to Brandy. Brandy reached down to pet Diego when Theo walked from his bedroom. Looking first at Cee and then Brandy, Theo's forehead squinched up.

"What's wrong?" Brandy said, stroking Diego's head.

"I thought you weren't coming back," Theo said to Brandy with an angry look. He looked over to Cee, now noticing his stance. "And what's wrong with you, big brother?"

"Well, we ran into some Underworld guards, and they didn't seem to friendly. I also found a painting - which I think came from my house in England." As Cee motioned toward the painting, Brandy looked at him, surprised.

"Can we go back now? You said we could go back," Brandy said, overcoming her shock and regaining her me, me, me, attitude.

Cee motioned toward Brandy as if to show Theo what he had been dealing with. Theo snorted a bit, as did Diego, but for different reasons. Brandy's hand had stopped on Diego's head as she spoke.

Theo looked over at Brandy. "And where is it you want to go?"

"I have to get word to my family. Our base was invaded by more than one outsider," she said, tossing a nasty glare at Cee.

"Remember, you started it," Cee bounced.

"Let me get Panterra. Underworld soldiers are nothing to play about, so let's go together. Jan is at the gate, and Meredith is doing witchy stuff. But first Cee, don't you want to put the collar back on Turk?" Theo nodded toward the statue.

Cee was torn. He wanted to, but he also wanted to help Brandy. He didn't know how long it may take Turk to come back after the collar was replaced. He did know they were on the clock with the guards sniffing around Brandy's family's property. *By the Gods, what is wrong with me?*

As if Theo could tell, he made the decision for him. "Panterra, come here."

The tall, thin, raven haired woman walked out of the same room Theo had appeared from. Wearing a pair of black jeans and a black tank top, she paused to put her hair into a pony tail. "Yeah? Oh, hey Cee and Brandy. Wait - why is she still here?" Panterra pointed at the red-haired woman.

"No offense, but I don't know why I'm here either. Cee dragged me through some portal, and well, here I am. I would have rather been left in Ireland," Brandy responded, feeling the unwelcoming air.

Panterra side-eyed Brandy while Cee responded to her questioning. "We ran into a little bit of an issue with some of our fellow guards while getting the collar. I told her I would go back to help her."

"Yup. And I told Cee we would go with him." Theo grinned when Panterra looked around wildly, confused.

"I doubt they are 'our fellow guards' considering most of our fellow guards fell in Thanatos' castle," Panterra said, squinting at Theo.

He shrugged in response with a smirk on his face.

Brandy looked between Panterra and Theo, trying to figure out what they were talking about. However, before she could say anything, Cee spoke up.

"Panterra please, we could use your help. You know I'm not the best in these situations," Cee said, almost pleading.

"Why does this matter so much to you? We have the collar. Just be done with her and let's move on." Theo nodded in agreement with Panterra.

Before Cee could respond, Brandy cleared her throat loudly. "Enough about whether I should be here or not. My family may be in danger, remember?"

Cee continued on after looking at Brandy like she hadn't interrupted them, "So, could this be Sopek's doing?" Cee asked.

"No. I'm sure he's dead. I have had Reapers asking me to claim his old contracts for some time now," Panterra answered.

"Someone had to send the guards after Brandy. Well, I guess we don't know for sure if they were after Brandy or after her family. We don't know what the end game is. Please, can you come with us as a personal favor to me?"

Cee rarely asked for favors, so when he did, she knew he was serious. The added emotion in his voice really gave her reason for alarm.

"Oh Panterra, I almost forgot. I ran into a friend of ours. Well, I'm not entirely sure it was our friend until I look into my books about it, but I think it was anyway. A redwood chair that bites?"

"That bastard is still around? I guess that gives me another reason to go to Dublin. I have a chair to burn." Panterra thought about it for a minute before deciding. "Well, by the Underworld, I haven't been to Dublin in what? Three months now?" Panterra looked at Theo. "Maybe we could get a drink at that pub you got drunk in when we were there last." All four turned toward Diego as he snorted at Panterra's comment.

"Oh, so funny, Reaper. I'm hurt." Theo mockingly put both hands over his heart. "But that does sound like a good idea.

Cee rolled his eyes at the display. "Are we going then? Diego, are you coming or are you staying?"

Brandy had never seen a dog look like it was pondering a question the way Diego was.

"He said he would rather stay home if that is okay. He's had enough of Dublin's pubs to last a lifetime," Theo answered for Diego.

Brandy looked between Diego, Theo, and Cee. *They're crazy. I'm surrounded by crazy people. He may have said he could talk to dogs, but I didn't believe him. And why did Theo just call Panterra 'reaper'?*

"Okay, then let's get a move on. Brandy, where are we going?"

"I live in Christchurch on Cathedral View Court," she replied.

"Umm, I have never been there," Cee said looking around.

"Oh, I believe I've been near there. Is there a pub named the Capstan Bar near your house, Brandy?"

"Yeah, it's just down the main street–maybe six blocks? We may see my Da or my brother Oran there. They both like that place."

"Then let's get going." Theo said as he opened the portal. Once it was opened, the group began to step through. This time Brandy kept her eyes open, but still reached for Cee's hand.

They walked out of the portal and looked around. They had appeared in an alley between two tall buildings. Theo made sure everyone was through the portal before stepping out into the street.

"I thought you were taking us to The Capstan Bar?" Panterra commented as she looked around.

"Oh wife. Ye of little faith, we are at the bar, just look." Theo waved his hand in front of him as he beckoned for the group to catch up.

As Panterra, Brandy, and Cee stepped onto the sidewalk, they saw Theo had indeed delivered them to the bar. To their left was a three-story brick building with "The Capstan Bar" in large letters.

"Only been here a couple of times eh?" Panterra asked as she brushed past Theo.

Rolling his eyes, Theo replied, "The number of times I have or have not been to this bar is not important. What is important is that I have delivered us to where I said I would."

Brandy looked at Cee, who just shrugged at Panterra and Theo's banter.

"Brandy, you know this area better than the rest of us, would you like to lead the way?" Panterra asked, ignoring Theo's comments.

"Sure, but let me check the bar real fast to see if Da or Oran are there." With that, Brandy disappeared for a minute before returning. "No luck, maybe they're at home." Brandy then looked both ways before walking across the street.

"After you." Theo motioned to Cee as he reached for Panterra's hand. To anyone who saw the four walking down the street, they would just assume it was a group of friends out for a daily stroll. The group followed Brandy down a side street and around another corner before stopping in front of a two-story brick house. The house was old, but you could see it was cared for. There was a black wrought iron fence with a small gate. Brandy took off, rushing through the gate toward the door.

"Brandy stop, we need to make sure it is safe."

Almost to the door, Brandy stopped and looked back, suddenly unsure.

"Maybe, I am starting to feel...strange?" she said stepping back.

Theo stretched before clapping his hands together. As he did so, a flash of blue appeared, quickly replaced by a pair of swords. "I got this." Walking through the small garden, he reached for the knob while holding both swords in one hand, but the door opened on its own. "Stay back."

Theo squatted down in an attack stance, swords out. Out from the darkness walked a gray and black cat. It paused slightly, looking at Theo before continuing out. "So, the cat opened the door? Really? Anyone else see this?" He looked back at the party for some recognition.

"It's okay. Big, strong Theo's going to protect us from the itty, bitty kitty." Panterra shook her head as she walked in ahead Theo.

"Will Theo and Panterra be okay?" Brandy looked at Cee, uncertainty in her eyes. The cat had begun to circle Brandy's legs before reaching up with its front paws in hopes of being picked up. Brandy cradled the cat before looking back at Cee. "I don't want them to hurt my family."

"They will be fine. They have survived some really trying times." Cee paused for a second, looking at the cat Brandy picked up. "They will only hurt those who deserve it. Your family will not be harmed."

Taking in what Cee had said, she turned back to the front door, as if willing something to happen.

Theo walked back out scowling. "Cee, I think you should see something. Brandy, can you please wait outside for a minute?"

"No, I'm going in. This is my house."

"Brandy, you can stay outside, or I can have Panterra force you to wait outside. Please, just for a minute," Theo practically pled with Brandy. He didn't want Panterra to have to hold the bounty hunter back, be he would if he had to.

"Fine, but I'm officially telling you I don't like it." Brandy stomped her foot, but rested against the fence with the cat in her arms.

As Cee walked in, he immediately knew why Theo wanted him to see inside the house. It was trashed. Every item in the house had been torn, ripped, cut, or broken. Someone was obviously looking for something. He had a sinking feeling he knew what it was, yet he didn't know why. After looking over the rest of the downstairs, he moved upstairs with Theo to see what Panterra found, if anything. As they walked into what looked like the master bedroom, they saw Panterra holding what appeared to be a photo frame. She stood next to a bed with a deep cut down the center and a smashed lamp laying on the bedspread.

"This was one of the only things I found that hadn't been completely destroyed," Panterra said while turning to face the guys. She handed the frame to Theo who looked at it briefly before handing it to Cee.

"Oh no." The words rushed from Cee's mouth as he studied the photo.

"What just happened?" Theo looked around for the cause of alarm.

"Oh, it seems I have finally put some facts together. I have to go speak to Brandy." Holding the frame close to his chest, he walked through the bedroom door. Theo and Panterra could hear his footsteps on the stairs.

Panterra and Theo just looked at each other before following him. As they reached the front door, they ran into Cee, who had stopped dead in his tracks.

"What in the Underworld, Cee? Why did you stop? I am tiring of your antics," Theo said upon regaining his balance after getting squished between Cee and Panterra

"Umm." Cee rotated slightly to allow Panterra and Theo a view of the front yard. They both understood what caused him to stop. Standing in the middle of the small garden was Brandy, breathing heavily. There was blood on her duster. In one hand was a short sword and in the other a dagger, both dripping with blood. At her feet lay what appeared to be four Underworld guards. Cee cautiously made his way to Brandy while Theo and Panterra rushed into the open yard, ready for the next attack.

"Brandy, what happened?" Cee asked as he neared the bodies. Seeing the fire in her eyes, he slowed until he was barely within arm's reach. As Cee lightly rested his hand on her cheek, his thumb wiped away a droplet of blood, almost as if she had been crying. As he gently wiped the blood, the fire in her eyes slowly died down, leaving only emerald green looking back at him. Cee realized he hadn't looked into those eyes before now. Yet they captivated him, holding his soul. Unable to look away, he just stood there feeling emotions he had thought forgotten.

Cybele had come to Hades bearing gifts for the Cerberus brothers before they were considered the dogs of the Underworld. He believed to her to be young, but he never knew her true age. She had brilliant red hair, green eyes as powerful as the ocean, and he had fallen head over heels for her. The gifts did not return to his memory, just her. Hades had introduced her to all three brothers over dinner. Cee loved the way her name had rolled off his tongue and wanted to spend as much time as he could with her.

He was pulled back from the memory by Brandy calling his name, "Cee are you okay? Hello."

He could hear her, and he regained his sense of time. "Brandy, Brandy, what happened? Are you hurt?" he asked, now looking at the dead soldiers.

"No, I don't think so. What got into you? You just froze. Do you have a thing with blood?" she whispered, not wanting to embarrass him.

Shaking off the question, he again asked, "What happened?"

Theo and Panterra walked up to the pair, looking at Cee. Theo shook his head, indicating all the guards were dead.

Cee had hoped one survived so they could have interrogated him. Cee assumed those who had trashed Brandy's house were working for the same boss, if not the same guys he had seen in the bounty trove. Cee walked over to the closest body and looked at the chest armor. Kneeling, he rolled the man over and brushed the bloody grass off the armor plate. He saw what looked to be a poorly drawn lion with snakes instead of a mane. He had never seen it before and looked at Theo and Panterra. "Have you seen this image before?"

Both Theo and Panterra shook their heads.

Brandy walked up to Cee and looked down. "I have seen that image. It was on some items my brother brought home a while back. A coin or amulet maybe? No definitely a coin. Oran was so excited about it, and he kept showing it off." She shrugged her shoulders.

Cee looked at her, amazed by how she had so easily handled herself and was now past the moment.

These guards are no slouches. They are usually trained by the best the gods have to offer. Considering they are used to fight the God's wars and defend their charges if need be, even to the death in many situations.

"Do you know of any Underworld bosses who mint their own coins?"

Again, Theo and Panterra were of no use as they shook their heads.

"Do you know why Underworld guards would be searching for something in your house? Did you keep objects or anything here?" Panterra asked, stepping forward to stand next to Brandy.

"Underworld guards? I don't know what you're talking about. Who are these people? And no, we never keep anything here. We always kept it at the trove, so we would be safe here. Why? Did something happen in the house?" Brandy said, eyeing her home.

Before anyone could stop her, Brandy rushed into the house. Knowing it was empty, the three let her go.

"You may want to go in there, Cee. She seems to like you," Panterra suggested after they heard a scream and then a sob.

"After what I have to tell her, I don't think she's going to like me anymore." Cee looked down at the photo frame still in his hand.

"Well, you can tell her that bit of info after we figure out what happened here. You said there were Underworld guards at the 'trove', as you and Brandy called it. Did you see the brand?"

"No, I stepped out long enough to notice they were Underworld guards and wanted to get her away from them."

Theo and Panterra shared a knowing glance that Cee missed while continuing to look at the photo frame.

"Well, let's assume for simplicity's sake these were the same guards, or maybe more guards from the same god. Why would a human family come under the scrutiny of the Underworld? They usually don't meddle with the younger souls," Theo said continuing to look at the strange symbol on the guard's chest plates.

"Guys, I don't think she's fully human. I felt something else. It was faint, like it was buried or inactive, but there is more there."

"No shit, Panterra. She just brought down Underworld guards by herself. I mean, that would have been easy for me, but how did she do it?" Theo said, turning to Cee.

Cee was thinking the same thing as Brandy walked out of the house, looking down while shuffling her feet.

"Who would do this? What did we do to someone? I mean, we have stolen items, but we have been doing that for years." For a second, Brandy blushed in embarrassment. "I mean, we returned them to their rightful owners from people who stole them first. Nothing that would have brought on something like this." As if she remembered something, she ran back into the house.

"So, if they haven't taken anything that would have prompted this, and I believe her, what did?" Cee asked anyone who was still listening.

"I have no idea, but boy did her family land on someone's radar." Theo nodded as Brandy ran back out holding a black notebook.

"Seriously you have a 'black book'?" Panterra rolled her eyes at the rudimentary object.

"Yes, but it isn't what you think. It isn't clients, but objects we have procured. We never write down a client's name or job. We only keep that information in our heads. It protects our clients and keeps enemies at bay—" Brandy looked back toward her house, "usually."

"Well, I guess small blessings and all that." Panterra was now curious as to the exact information the book held. She walked over to Brandy as she opened the book. Skimming over the entries, Panterra nodded here and there, and raised her eyebrows at a couple of entries. "I agree, I don't think there is anything that would have prompted the Underworld gods to search for something here. Mostly just antiques and other strange objects. Overall, this is impressive. I think there even are some items you used to own in here Theo." Panterra patted Brandy's shoulder before rejoining Theo, who was now looking quite interested in the book.

"Brandy, before we dive too far into the book, how did you bring these guards down?" Cee asked, looking her over again and surprised to find no obvious wounds.

"Well, I mean, it wasn't that hard." With that, Brandy began to explain what happened while the three were inside the house.

7

Brandy watched Cee join Theo and Panterra inside the house immediately after refusing to let her into her own home. Figuring it was something Cerberus-y, she leaned against the fence railing. She looked down at her nails on one hand, while holding the cat with the other. Seeing her nails were trashed, Brandy considered how quickly she could get an appointment with the lady down the street. She was great about making same day appointments. *Maybe Panterra would like to accompany me. She isn't horrible.* Brandy was great at keeping her nails looking good, regardless of what nasty things she encountered during her jobs. She wondered if Cee liked long nails or short. She looked up as she heard a noise to her left. *Had Cee or Theo come around from the side?* As she watched the individual walk around the side of the house, she realized it was not one of the brothers or Panterra. It appeared to be a guy wearing a hooded black cape with bronze armor and a golden symbol centered on the chest piece. She couldn't see his face but she could see the sword in his hand. From the look of the man and his sword, she could guess his reach and waited for him to make a move.

Putting down the cat, Brandy reached behind her back with her right hand while still pretending to not notice the approaching threat. Her hand rested on the handle of the dagger she had taken from her room. Hoping he hadn't noticed her small movements, she let him come closer. Brandy closed her eyes and focused on her other senses. She could hear his footfalls on the grass even has he tried to be stealthy. She could even hear his steady breathing as he came closer. Oh, he has no idea I know he's there. She continued to play the game by humming an old tune she remembered from when she was young. It was a lullaby her brother used to sing to her that he had learned from their mother.

I wonder where my family is and if they are okay. She let her thoughts drift for a second, but only a second. Soon, she could sense he was close. Her grip on the dagger tightened and when she opened her eyes, she was staring straight into solid dark orbs. Quickly, she slashed her right arm out and around, catching him in the throat with the tiny but sharp blade. At the same time, she side-stepped and heard the harmless thud of the assailant's sword hitting the grass.

Not knowing if her cut was deep enough, she approached his body. She nudged his body a couple of times to see if he would move. When he didn't, she stepped away and returned to her spot at the fence. Assuming he was not alone, she kept her mind focused and waited.

Within a minute or two, three more guards walked around the house following the same path as the first. Each wielding a similar sword and wearing the same armor. Knowing she couldn't play the helpless damsel this time, she prepared for a fight. She switched the dagger into her off hand and pulled a short sword from her belt. The three guards instantly saw the fourth on the ground as they turned the corner and pulled their weapons immediately.

The three spread out, coming at Brandy from three different directions. Again, she closed her eyes, slowed her breathing, and focused her thoughts. Her Da had taught her to fight, but she started to beat him when she was ten. He blamed it on his getting older, but after she started beating him, he would never let her fight her brothers either. Well that wasn't entirely true. Her Da let her fight Colin, her middle brother, but she could never fight Flannigan, the oldest.

As the three approached her, she chose her attack. When the first guard to her right got close enough, she kicked out her leg and caught her victim on the side of the knee. She knew it was broken because she heard the crack as her boot made contact. Before he hit the ground, she used him as a step to jump over the second, leaving the short sword in the second guard's neck. Turning around, she wrapped her arm around his chest, turning them both toward the third, and untouched guard. Quickly, she pushed the body of the second guard into the third. As he fell, she removed her sword that had been in his neck. The dead weight knocked the third guard back.

She turned her attention toward the first guard again, who had made his way to his feet. His sword was heavier, and with a broken knee, it took him longer to catch up to Brandy as she parried one swing from his sword. She dogged the second before invading his defense and embedding her dagger into his side with the precision of an assassin. Blood pooled around his body while she focused her attention back on the third guard as he regained his footing.

Taking a running start, she slid on the now wet grass under the wide arc of the man's steel sword. As she passed, her sword caught his upper thigh leaving a line of new blood. He stumbled forward and used his sword to keep from falling. Lifting his sword, he held it over his head.

"Seriously, did they send the B team? Because you guys are dying pretty fast."

The guard growled at her insult and rushed forward. He was fast but Brandy was faster. She brought her sword around, and he defended the slash with his own. The clang of steel sang in the quiet yard. As the swords touched, she kicked his sword wielding elbow with her left leg, knocking the sword free. Shaking his head, he began to rush her, hoping to disarm the infuriating woman and teach her a lesson. As he got closer, she dropped down. When he was close enough, she stood, using his body weight to propel him over her.

As he fell, she and walked over to his dropped sword. Picking it up and testing the balance, she turned toward the guard. She threw her dagger, which hit him in the shoulder and knocked him back slightly. While he was focusing on getting the dagger out of his shoulder, she walked up and stabbed him in the leg with his own blade. Grabbing the dagger, she ripped it out and nonchalantly used the guards coat to wipe his own blood off the blade. "So, B team it was. Tsk, tsk, tsk. Guess your boss thought you were expendable."

Standing back, she contemplated the guard in front of her. She doubted he even knew anything aside from, 'go, find, kill, maim' from the boss.

"So, have anything to say?"

"Pfft, you know nothing, Demi. Maybe you should be looking a bit closer to home," the man said calmly while struggling to stand with a blade in his leg.

Brandy didn't know what the guard meant by Demi, but it sounded like a slur of some sort. *Maybe he thinks I'm someone else? But who else?* He must not know anything about her. But he would in a minute. Before she could speak again, the man pulled his own sword from his leg and fell on it.

She stood back, her own blades still in hand, amazed at what she had just seen. His lifeless body on the ground, answers dying with him. She stopped and looked around when she heard another noise. Standing in the doorway was Cee.

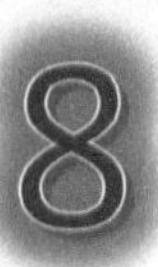

"Where did you learn to fight?" Panterra asked as the others were going through the guard's coats, looking for any clue as to why they were there.

"My Da taught me the basics when I was a kid. I used to fight with him and my two brothers, but it wasn't long before I was beating Da and Oran every time. Then they just stopped practicing with me. Colin would let me battle him since I didn't beat him all the time, but I think when I was young, he used to let me win. He could hold his own. I think my Da and older brother were jealous of him."

"You love your family; I can see it. I never knew my family. I was taken when I was young and spent most my life in the furnace. I hope we can find them," Panterra replied as she walked back to Theo.

Holding the photo frame he had taken from upstairs, Cee replaced Panterra.

"I have something I need to tell you. It might sound strange, and you won't want to believe me, but what I'm about to tell you is the truth."

Brandy didn't know what Cee was about to tell her, but she knew it was serious.

"I know you may still be confused about what Theo and I do, or Panterra for that matter. I will give you the quick and dirty so you can better understand the truth." Cee hated explaining who he was, but sometimes it was necessary. Theo and Jan were so much better with interpersonal relationships. Meredith would have known how to approach these topics, but she wasn't here either.

Cee began his explanation of who he was. "We don't know how old we are. We don't know a lot, but we are the guardians to the gate of the Underworld."

Theo gave a little wave.

"No way. You mean like Satan?"

"What? No, he lives in Wisconsin. Actually, he runs a cheese shop. We are the guardians Cerberus. You know, like with Hades?" he said, picking his words carefully.

"So, you are talking about mythology. That's not real," she said still confused.

"Sort of. Actually, all myth is based in fact, it just gets a little tweak over time. Like the legends of Cerberus." She shrugged, so he continued, "The guardian of the Underworld, Hades', three-headed dog. Well, our last name is Cerberus, and there are three of us. Also, we mostly have had dogs as companions. You get the connection now?" he asked.

Brandy, still trying to grasp what he was telling her, had so many questions. "Okay, so you guard the gates to the Underworld. That means what exactly?"

"Simply, we help Reapers." Cee motioned to Panterra, who waved. "We usher souls who have reached, or are near to reaching, their awareness to the Underworld. After that, we don't know what happens. Those who are capable are released to find their own way, but that is really not our focus."

"Okay, but why are you telling me this?" she said, shifting her weight to a defensive stance.

"Oh. Don't worry. We have moved past killing you, darling," Panterra chimed in, seeing her change in posture.

Cee took a step toward Brandy, sorrow heavy in his eyes before looking at her. "Remember the day we brought you to that cavern? The cavern was the gateway. If you hadn't noticed, the Gate itself was there in the background the whole time. Giant stone, strange writing. Well, I was at work that day, with Theo's dog Diego. We had an incident with a soul who kept trying to escape. The soul mentioned something about a daughter who was a bounty hunter and said she was in danger. We deal with souls with bad excuses and begging all the time so I didn't think a lot about it."

Brandy brought her dagger out and backed away from him. "You...You knew who I was, and you played along? You killed my father? How could you look at me with warm eyes and yet be so cold?"

Cee put both of his hands up, still holding the frame in one hand. "It's okay, but I have to explain the whole thing. Brandy, trust me, if I knew he was your father, I would have told you right away. In fact, I may have even said something just to hurt you more in the beginning."

Tears were forming on Brandy's lower eyelid, and when she blinked, they rolled down her cheek.

"Something kept tugging at my memory, but it wasn't until I was upstairs and saw the image of your family here," Cee handed Brandy the photo frame, "that I realized it was your father who had come through."

"But you said the soul shouldn't have been there. What did you mean by that?"

Cee saw Theo and Panterra's attention was also now focused on what Cee was about to say.

"The reaper came in with a plane accident, 100 souls on board. However, when we counted the coins, there were 202. There should only have been 200. We didn't think much of it until a male soul took off, and Diego had to corral him." Cee paused to allow Brandy to take in the information.

"Did the Reaper know where the soul came from?" Panterra broke the silence.

"He did not. In fact, he was worried you would take his scythe."

"I would never…okay, I likely would, but not in this case. But you say it was one of my wards?" Panterra was now almost buzzing with impatience.

"Yes. Male reaper, nice, kept calling me Master Cee. I told him to knock it off," Cee replied before turning his attention back to Brandy. "I'm sorry I didn't know he was your father. If I had, I would have told you sooner, I do not keep secrets. It seemed like your father had some regrets. Regrets of not being able to see you finish your first bounty. He thought you may be in trouble and was worried about you. I know it's sad, but you have to know he did not want to enter the gate."

"While I would love to sit around and mourn the loss of my father, I still have two brothers, and maybe even a mother out there who may need my help." With that, she walked back into the house.

Cee didn't know whether or not to follow her, but Panterra walked up to him.

"Don't worry, she is strong," she told him before following Brandy into the house.

"Dude, she is a *beast*. She killed four guards in a relatively short amount of time, all by herself, I might add. Her father being an unknown soul is concerning though. Why is all this happening now? It seems like someone in the Underworld is making a play, we just don't know what," Theo said sounding surprised.

"I know. And with her brothers missing, I have a feeling they play a role in this as well. I just don't know how much. This is something we need bring to Jan's attention," Cee responded. "There is something else I didn't tell Brandy. I don't really understand it myself but you may. When I went to her after she killed the guards, I looked into her eyes. There were something familiar about them."

"Well duh, you *have* been spending quite a bit of time with her lately, so it would not surprise me that they look familiar," Theo retorted.

"No Theo, I don't think you understand. Remember when Hades introduced us to Cybele while we were still in Greece? The redhead who had a gift for us. Do you remember her?" Cee asked Theo.

"It's vaguely familiar, but there is no way Cybele is Brandy. She' is way too young and way to human to be a soul we met all that time ago. I don't remember a gift though. What was the gift?"

"That is just it, I can't remember any details. It all seems cloudy. I remember meeting her, wanting to spend time with her, but after that it goes fuzzy. The next thing I remember is working with Targus at the gate. This was all before you met Panterra. You can't tell me you don't remember any of that."

"Cee, like I said, I vaguely remember, but it isn't really clear. We have lived so many lives it's hard to piece together anything from those days," Theo said, shrugging his shoulders.

Before Cee could say anything else, Panterra and Brandy reappeared with two bags.

"Umm, what's going on here?" Theo asked, reaching for the bag Panterra was carrying.

"Well, since we may have gotten Brandy into this, I figured we would have her stay at the house with us while we figure everything out." Panterra briefly winked at Theo.

"WHAT? Absolutely not. We didn't get her into anything. She started it, remember? I won't stay with her in the house. She's still trouble," Cee said it reflexively, but his heart was not in his words.

"Oh Underworld, Cee, give it up, okay? She needs a place until we figure out why the guards are after her. With our current schedule, we can rotate who helps us and who works the gate."

Like a whiny child, Cee turned around and kicked at the ground. He had lost Turk but had gained this dynamic bounty hunter. He wanted his life to be back the way it was. With Turk at his side being logical, and Cee not having romantic feelings toward someone. Turning back around, he regained his composure. "I'm sorry for the outburst. Upon further consideration, I think her staying at the house would be best to help and understand the predicament we seem to be in."

"Okay, whatever. It's settled then. Theo can you conjure up a way home? I want to get back to sunny Oregon. This cloudy weather is making my hair frizz out," Panterra said, patting her raven hair.

Theo sidled up to Panterra. "I thought you liked Dublin?"

Panterra rolled her eyes while Brandy laughed. "Yeah, when it's sunny."

Theo laughed and opened the portal.

Brandy reached for Cee's hand. "Look, I'm sorry for what I did. At the time, I didn't know you or your brothers. It was just a job. A job I now know wasn't the best idea. Will you please forgive me?"

Cee looked into Brandy's eyes before focusing on her whole face. "Let's just get home, get this collar back on, and go from there, okay?" Cee still believed he could place the collar back on Turk and Turk would come back to life.

Arriving a short time later in Oregon, Cee took off toward the door, the mission of bringing Turk back on his mind.

Panterra, Theo, and Brandy all looked at each other with worried looks.

"It didn't fucking work," yelled Cee from the living room.

All three rushed into the living room to find Cee kneeling in front of the statue, the blue woven material strung around Turk's neck, and the stone hanging low.

"Wait, this is Turk? This isn't the dog I took the collar from. Although now that I look at it, it does kind of look like him."

"No, you idiot, it's him." Cee stood and started toward Brandy again. Panterra stepped between them.

"Cee, did you ever explain to Brandy what happened? Or did it cross your mind that not everyone knows everything?"

Looking down at his feet, Cee looked back up. "I figured she knew. She was there when he turned."

"Well whatever it is, I didn't know." Brandy stepped out from behind Panterra and reached for Cee. "Please tell me what is going on?"

"Do you remember the night you took the collar? Did you notice anything weird with the Doberman after you took the collar off of him?"

"Um, no, not really." With that, Brandy started her side of the events leading up to Turk's transformation.

Arriving at the large house, Brandy looked around and saw only two cars in the driveway. Which according to her observations, meant one brother was gone. Which likely meant maybe the dog was gone as well. She also knew from the layout one brother and his wife lived in the adjoining house, so they shouldn't hear her enter. Hopefully, the brother who was gone was the one who lived with the dog.

Approaching the door, Brandy reached for the knob to see if it was unlocked. Surprisingly, it was but she guessed if there were at least three people and a dog living in a house, you have constant security. She opened the door slowly and looked around. With the lights off, all she could see was the living room illuminated by the dim light coming from the fireplace.

Near the fireplace, laid a large Doberman who looked up when she entered. Assuming he would sound the alarm, she put her finger to her lips. *Brandy it's a dog. It doesn't understand what you just did.* But for some reason, the dog just looked at her with his head cocked to the side as if trying to figure out what was going on, but not worried. She felt as though he was looking into her soul.

Pulling out her dagger in case she had to use it, she walked into the middle of the living room. The dog came up to her and rubbed against her leg. She reached down to pet him and that's when she saw the collar. Remembering what the instructions had said about watching out for the dog, she reached down to touch it. At first touch, a jolt of power jumped from the collar to her and shocked her hand away. The dog just continued to look at her like it knew what she was going to do, and he was fine with it. Not seeing any of the brothers burst into the room, she reached for the collar and undid the clasp. With the collar off, the dog calmly sat down. Patting him on his head one more time, Brandy looked around the house quickly for anything of immediate worth. Seeing nothing, she turned and slowly closed the door behind her.

***

What she had not seen was Meredith in the shadows by the door that connected the two houses. As Brandy jogged away, Meredith silently followed at a distance. To Meredith, Brandy appeared to have a red aura around her, making it very easy to track her.

***

"Lies. Turk wouldn't have just sat down for you while you killed him."

"Are you listening to yourself? I did not kill him. I took his collar and left unseen. Well, at least I thought I was unseen at the time."

Exasperated, Cee finally walked over to Brandy and led her to near the statue. "Brandy, this statue is Turk. It doesn't just look like him, it is him."

"What? No! When I left, he was just sitting there. He was warm when I patted his head before leaving."

"Well, between the time you left and when Cee came out of his room, Turk's body transformed from the warm, furry Doberman body to this cold, stone statue," Panterra tried to explain.

"But…no, I didn't mean for that to happen. Wait, why did that happen? How could that happen?"

Cee and Theo looked at each other, silently debating whether to tell her everything. Even though Cee had thrown a fit about Brandy staying at their house, in his deepest of hearts, he was happy about it.

Realizing since they were in for a penny, they may as well be in for a pound, Cee explained what he had witnessed when he came out of his room.

***

Cee had heard what sounded like Turk or another dog circling on the couch, getting ready for a long nap as he tried to find the shirt he was looking for. It was one of his favorites and for some reason, he had a drive to wear it. He figured Turk was just moving around. Probably moving from in front of the fireplace to one of the couches, which he did frequently when he got too warm.

It had been quiet with Theo out of town helping Panterra with her issue, and so Cee and Turk had been relaxing before Jan invited Cee out to dinner. Which brought him to his closet trying to find that shirt.

"Hey Turk, have you seen that black Hard Rock shirt I like?" Cee shouted out of the room. When he initially did not hear a response, he thought nothing of it. Sometimes Turk would ignore him, even if he was awake, and there was a good chance he was sleeping. He wasn't that old, but Cee had noticed him slowing down a bit lately. Finally finding the shirt, Cee put it on and walked into the dining room. The living room was dark save for the glow of the fireplace. His hand felt around on the wall until he found the familiar knob. The light burst through the room sending the darkness into hiding.

What he saw confused him. Was one of his brother's playing a joke? There, near the door was a perfect replica of Turk in stone form. Looking around for the living Turk, Cee realized he didn't see him.

"Turk, where are you?" Nothing. Dead silence was all Cee heard. Honestly, Cee couldn't remember the last time it had been this long since he had heard a dog talking inside his head. For most of his dogs, it was non-stop. Turk, however, usually only spoke when it was necessary. But now there was nothing. …

"Turk? Where are you, boy?" Cee walked toward the door to Jan's wing. "Hey Jan, Meredith, have you seen Turk?"

Jan opened the door, drying off his hair from a shower. "Umm, no, he isn't in here that I know of. Let me ask Sammie and Meredith."

Turning around Jan yelled, "Sammie, Meredith, have you seen Turk?"

"Well that's odd. Meredith isn't answering me either. Sammie says she has no idea, but she will come sniff it out if she needs to. Although she says she is comfy on the couch and so only if she has to," Jan replied with a roll of his eyes. Sammie was a female Boxer who was about 7 years old. She was a little bit older than Diego but still younger than Turk.

"So, you're saying you didn't have anything to do with the statue in the living room?"

Jan sighed, practical jokes were Theo's thing, and Theo was gone. "Cee, I honestly have no idea what you're talking about. Come show me."

As Cee walked Jan over to the statue, Sammie came prancing into the room. She walked up to the statue and sniffed it. Then she rubbed her body against it like it was a tree.

"Cee, Sammie says that is definitely Turk. She can smell the foo-foo doggy shampoo you use for him."

"What? He has sensitive skin. But she must be wrong, this can't be him."

"Whatever. She says it's him, and if you hadn't noticed, his collar is gone." Sammie walked back into Jan's wing, likely to sit on the couch again now that the task was over. She even had a blanket she would wiggle under when it got cold.

"What? How is the collar gone? And where is Meredith?" Jan held up his hand as Cee asked the question, already on the phone.

"Meredith, where did you go? Call me when you get this, please? Something has happened to Turk." Jan faced Cee. "I don't know where she is, and she's not answering her phone. Oh, let me check the 'find my app'." Jan had required all the family, including Panterra and Meredith, to add the app to their phones. It was annoying, but for times like this it was beneficial.

After 30 seconds of tapping, Jan finally looked up. "Her location isn't available. Do you think Meredith is in trouble? Maybe she was turned into stone somewhere else."

Cee walked up to Jan and put his arm around his shoulder. "No, her phone would have still worked. I'm sure she's okay. But we need to figure this out!" he shouted, pointing to Turk. As he said it, a tear slid down his face.

It was Jan's turn to console Cee. "We will figure this out, I promise you."

Right as Cee sat down on the couch to think about everything going on, the front door opened to Theo and Panterra laughing.

10

"So, I did hurt him? I didn't mean to, Cee. I swear, I really didn't know it would hurt him." Brandy walked up to where Cee had sat down while telling his story.

"I believe you, but now the collar won't work. It isn't bringing him back. I don't understand why," Cee said reliving the pain and heartbreak anew.

No one spoke as they all looked between Cee and the statue.

"Is there anything special you're supposed to say when you transfer the collar between the old dog and the new one?" Panterra asked, hoping it would help him think about options.

"No, I just do it. Could it have been because I didn't take it off? Why did he just let her take it? I just don't understand." Cee lowered his head into his hands in defeat.

"Can I try it?" Brandy asked. "Maybe since I was the one who took it off, I have to be the one who puts it back on?" Brandy said, her voice hopeful.

Cee looked up at Brandy and handed her the collar. "If you want to try, go for it, but I doubt it will do any good."

While she took the collar and sat next to Turk, Panterra noticed the painting they had taken from Brandy's room still leaning up against the side of the couch.

"What is this?" Panterra asked the group.

"It's a painting we grabbed when we escaped Brandy's stone 'storage unit'," Cee replied.

"Cee, didn't you notice what the man creature is holding?" Panterra asked, bending close to the image.

"Yeah, Brandy mentioned it was—well she thought it was—a stone like the one in the collar," Cee said uninterested.

Panterra picked up the painting and put it down right in front of Cee. "It doesn't look like the stone? I would bet my scythe it is the stone."

"It's just a painting," Cee said, rolling his eyes at Panterra.

"Seriously, it's the stone. Who is the painting of?" Panterra asked.

Cee looked at the painting again. "That's Fenrir. He was a creator of objects and stuff. He was killed a long time ago."

Brandy perked up. She had been sitting near the statue putting the collar onto Turk and then taking it off again, hoping one of the times, it would bring him back. She moved over to the painting, brushing her shoulder against Cee's leg.

"That's it. I didn't think about it when you told me the story before. I think I know this guy," she said, pointing at the central figure.

Cee looked at her strangely, as did Theo and Panterra. "How would you know him? He died during the Titan Wars, or Dryad Wars. Well, one of them anyway."

"No, I really think this is one of my clients. Let me think for a second." Brandy sat back and closed her eyes. As she did, she started to remember a past job.

***

It was two years ago when Brandy and Colin were sitting in their living room watching some inane reality show waiting for a job to arrive. Oran and their Da were on two different jobs; one was some object hunt, and the other was a bounty of some human criminal.

"I don't know why you like watching this crap, Brandy. It's so stupid," Colin said as he reached for the remote.

"Says the guy who has mainlined the last ten episodes with me?" Brandy smirked as she handed over the popcorn.

"I was keeping you company. Yeah, that's what it is." Colin said defending himself.

"Uh huh, whatever you say," she jabbed back at him.

Just then, Colin's phone beeped, indicating a secure message was on their server.

"Is that a job? Can I come with you? Please, I am so bored." Brandy almost jumped over the couch to read over Colin's shoulder.

"By Odin, stop for a minute, and let me read." Colin continued to read the message.

"Okay, so it looks like this guy named Fenn needs us to go to Egypt and get this rock that was embedded in a sarcophagus. He said it fell into the hands of a bad guy who would sell it to us for...looks like about ten thousand bitcoin, which Fenn has already wired to us. He says the guy should be easy to work with, but to make sure we don't mention his name at all or that it's for a job. We are to make up some excuse about why we want it."

"Buying things is your specialty, making up stories is mine." Brandy puffed out her chest with pride.

Colin had to agree, Brandy was good at making up stories on the fly, stories he believed even after he knew the truth.

"Okay, I'm guessing you want to come with me?" Colin looked over at her.

"Of course. When do we leave? I'm about done with TV for the next decade," Brandy said as she switched off the show.

"Well, let me call the guy and then if he agrees to it, we can catch the next flight to Cairo," Colin said as he typed the number into his phone.

"WOOHOO I haven't been to Egypt yet. This should be fun," Brandy called to her brother as he walked into the next room to call the number Fenn had given them for the seller.

Brandy could only hear snippets of their conversation as she started packing for the trip. Looking at her phone, she brought up the weather conditions for Cairo. *Oooo maybe we could stay a couple of extra days. I really want to check out the pyramids while we are there.* Seeing the weather was going to be warm, she packed light and hoped they would be staying at a hotel with a pool. She hated traveling with her Da because he always picked the most basic hotels. No room service, no maids, no pool. Sometimes there wasn't even food. Oran liked things much fancier. They would stay at 4 or 5-star hotels and be waited on like royalty. She felt that was a bit more than she needed though, which is why she liked traveling with Colin. He was simple, but still liked nice things.

As Brandy heard him hang up, she rushed back downstairs. "So, are we going? Say we are going. I already packed."

Colin chuckled. "Yes, we are going. Do you want to book the flights? Fenn has us on an expense account according to the message. So if you want to, go ahead and log in and get the information. I'm going to pack and leave a message for Oran and Da."

"Don't forget, I don't have my own account…still." This was a sore spot for Brandy because she felt old enough and experienced enough to have her own account.

"Just use mine then, I know you have the information." Came the reply from the other room. Brandy did have Colin's information, he had given it to her, but she was unsure why she couldn't have her own. Brandy had Oran's, but she had watched him put it in one night when she was much younger, and he never changed his passwords. Logging in, she retrieved the information she needed before logging off again.

"Colin, I ordered the tickets and reserved a hotel for two nights. I told them we may be there longer for vacation, but just two nights for right now."

"Sounds good. I'm ready. when does the plane leave?" he asked, walking out with two bags in tow.

"It leaves in four hours from Dublin International. We have time to go to the trove before heading out if we need to."

Colin walked down the stairs shaking his head. "I don't think we'll need to. Based on the way the message read and how the guy sounded like on the phone, this should be an easy acquire and deliver. You sure you want to come?"

"And miss a trip to Egypt? Forget about it, I'm coming." Brandy grabbed her backpack and her laptop from the side table before walking out the door to wait for the Uber.

Colin just shook his head and followed her.

Colin was right, the job was simple. In fact, it seemed too simple to Brandy. That was okay though because Fenn had said they could stay a couple of extra days on the expense account. So, Brandy had convinced her brother to stay the extra couple of days. They had updated Oran and Da about their status and spent the two extra days relaxing.

"So where do we deliver the gem to now that we have it?" Brandy asked her brother over a drink by the pool.

"When we have the plane information, I'm supposed to update Fenn. He said there would be a car to pick us up from the airport."

"Sounds good, now let me relax." Both Brandy and Colin laughed and continued to enjoy the Egyptian weather.

***

When Brandy and Colin touched down in Dublin, they were greeted by a young woman carrying a white board with their names on it. Walking up to her, Colin introduced himself, and they followed the her to a black town car.

I could get used to this type of treatment. Brandy thought to herself

As if her brother could read her thoughts, he took that moment to let her know she shouldn't get used to it.

After what seemed like a hundred hours of driving from the city into the countryside, they arrived at the remains of a castle. It wasn't dilapidated, but just rather small. As the car door opened, the driver instructed them to go through the main set of doors. Someone would be there to greet them. With that, she got back into the car and drove off.

The main doors had wolf shaped door knockers and beautiful bronze handles. Colin knocked lightly and then pushed slightly. Even though the doors stood at least eight feet tall, they opened with barely a sound. The foyer in front of them had a rich, dark wood floor with lighter colored walls. As they stepped in, a man in leather pants and a smock covering his shirt appeared from the back of the foyer. He was breathing heavily and a sheen of sweat glistened on his forehead, as if he had just ran there.

"Greetings. Follow me, please. The master is working, so hopefully loud noises don't bother you."

Both Colin and Brandy shook their heads and followed the individual down what Brandy thought was a never-ending set of stairs. No wonder the man was sweating, these stairs would kill just about anyone. Finally reaching the bottom, a doorway opened into a medium size room. A wooden worktable ran three quarters of the way around a stone forge. A fire crackled lighting a tall man who stood staring into the flames.

"You must be Colin and Brandy. It is a pleasure to finally meet you," the man said, still facing away from them.

Colin stepped forward. "It is a pleasure to meet you as well. We have your item." He never knew exactly what to say in front of others besides the client.

"You can speak freely in front of Blane. He has been my assistant for a very long time."

"Okay, well, we have the gem you requested."

Finally, Fenn turned around, his mouth momentarily parted in shock. He quickly regained himself and stepped forward toward Brandy. "My apologizes, but you are the splitting image of someone I knew very long ago."

"Hopefully it was someone good," Brandy spoke up. Colin glared at her for opening her mouth, but she didn't care. Why should she care? He had already paid, and she wasn't going to keep her mouth shut just because she may offend him.

Responding to Brandy, "Oh, she was. She was very good. In fact, I entrusted her with something of value." With that, he took the blue stone from Colin's hand and lifted it to the light. "This is exactly the stone I was looking for, many thanks." He turned back toward his forge and started working on the stone. He brought a giant hammer down on the rock over and over. Brandy was waiting for it to shatter, but it never did.

Blane stepped forward. "The car is waiting for you, and the fee for completion of the job has been delivered."

With one final look at Fenn, Brandy and Colin started the climb back up to the main floor of the building. Brandy thought it was a lot of work for the small amount of conversation, but the money in the bank made it worth it.

***

"Colin and I had a job awhile back where we had to get a stone for this rich guy in Ireland from this slimy guy in Egypt. As I remember, the man looked a lot like this one. In fact I really think this is the same guy we got that stone for. I wish Colin was here. He is much better with faces than I am."

"If what you are saying is true, then that means he did not die at the hands of Vioarr, as we always thought. Oh, Underworld. What a mess this could become if his existence becomes known. Can you just imagine what Odin would say?" Theo began to pace across the living room.

"Why is this a big deal? So, the dude faked his death. It happens more often than people realize. What do you mean by 'what Odin would say?' You all realize that Odin is a myth, right? Like, not a real person." Brandy was curious as to what other crazy fantasies the brothers would cook up. Brandy wondered if she really wanted to know.

"A myth like Fenrir, the half god, half wolf you worked for is, right?" Theo stopped in front of Brandy.

"No, he was just a man. There's no such thing as Gods. It's just a way for people to explain the unexplainable," Brandy said, suddenly unsure of her words.

"Theo, I think we need to tell Hades about this. We are going to be visiting someone who shouldn't be alive. It could create a whole new mess if the other gods find out, and it could be our necks on the line," Cee said matter of factly.

"Cee, I think you're right. Ugh, let me call Jan." With that, Theo walked out of the room.

11

"So, you are saying Fenrir is alive? After Odin told his own son, Vioarr, to kill Fenrir?" Hades asked as he poured another round of drinks.

"It would appear so. Not only that, but we need to have a conversation with Fenrir. The collar isn't bringing Turk back, and with the Underworld guards sniffing around Brandy's house, we think this may tie into Theo and Panterra's recent trip to Egypt to meet up with Sopek," Cee relayed to their boss.

Hades looked over the group sitting around the banquet table before speaking. "Okay. Jan, you need to stay. I not only need you at the gate, but it is the busy season for the vineyard. Cee, can you explain to Sherri what you need her to do to keep the wheels on while you are gone? Theo, you can do your job from anywhere, so you can go."

Brandy just sat back and watched. This man was the so-called God of the Underworld. And he was giving out orders like a normal business owner. *The God of the Underworld, nah, no way*, she thought. Honestly, her mind couldn't grasp what was going on.

"And as for you, do you want to go with them? We can set you up a job here at the vineyard and keep you safe while they are away." Hades directed his question at Brandy.

"No. I mean, no sir. Thank you, but I would like to go with them. Especially since I have met Fenrir before, so that may make it easier to get him to see us," Brandy said stiffly at being the direction for Hades question.

Hades laughed. "Yup, just like her. Not only do you look like Cybele, but you sound like her too. Okay then, well, I can't make you stay. Nor can I give you permission to go, so do what you may. But know the rest are under my protection. So, if you are planning on backstabbing or anything else underhanded, I will find out about it. And there will be dire consequences. Remember I am the God of the Underworld."

"Oh, oh no, I would never do that. It would not be beneficial," Brandy said gaining confidence.

Still laughing, Hades dismissed them. "Yup, just like her. Well, you'd best get ready. And please try not to cost me a lot of money. I am trying to run a business here."

***

That left Jan alone with Sammie and Meredith as Diego decided he wanted to meet Fenrir in the flesh instead of just hearing about it.

Brandy couldn't directly place the building on a map because the car's windows had been tinted, and she had not been paying attention. Just thinking about that last trip made Brandy sad. She still had not heard from anyone in her family, and she was starting to worry. Were her siblings dead like her Da was? She asked Jan and Theo if either had seen them come through the gate. Both shook their heads. Assuming they were as observant as Cee, she believed them.

Upon arriving in a field similar to the one Cee and Brandy had arrived in earlier in the month, they found their bearings and began to walk toward the nearest town. Cee and Theo both looked like they were ready for the office. On the other hand, Panterra was in all black with a heavy hooded cape and Brandy was still sporting her leather duster. They were an odd mix for sure, but no one seemed to mind them as they passed through two small hamlets on the way to town. While they walked the 10 miles to the town they were seeking, they talked about Brandy's childhood and what fun things there were to do around Dublin.

Once they got to town, Brandy asked a local innkeeper if they knew about the building she had visited. The first two had not, but the third knew exactly where she was talking about and showed her on a map. It wasn't far by foot, so the group decided rather than portaling again, they would walk.

Just before dusk, they arrived at the castle Brandy had described. Knocking on the door, Theo and Cee stood in front of the two ladies and dog. Diego sometimes scared people, and they didn't know what could be coming toward them when the door opened. As it opened, Brandy gasped, pushed through the brothers, yelling Colin at the same time as she jumped into the arms of the individual. Cee felt a pang of jealousy as he saw her in the arms of another man.

Theo looked at Cee and chuckled when he saw him looking so upset. Cee was about to ask Theo what he found so funny when he saw the face of the stranger holding Brandy. It was the male version of her. The hair, eyes, and even freckles were the same.

This must be one of her brothers. Wow am I stupid, or apparently love sick? Cee thought.

Brandy turned toward the group. "Everyone, this is my brother, Colin. Colin, this is everyone." Colin bowed slightly and let them in.

The moment the front door closed, Brandy began to pelt her brother with questions. "When did you arrive here? Why are you here? Did you know Da is dead? Do you know I look like someone named Cybele? Did you know they ransacked our house?"

Through all the questions, Colin just listened as they wound their way through the halls into a spacious library. "In time, Branda -Lynn. Please stay here, I will get Fenrir," was all Colin said before he turned and walked out the door.

"Branda -Lynn?" Cee asked while trying to hide the smile forming.

"Yeah, what of it, Caiaphas?" Brandy rose her chin as she shot back.

"How do you know that?" Cee asked giving her a quick glance.

"Oh, Panterra and I have had plenty of time to talk about you." Brandy grinned, showing all her teeth. It was slightly creepy to Cee and made his skin crawl, but he didn't know why.

He had come to realize she was much more than just some bounty hunter. Even after learning about Cee and his brothers, she was still standing toe to toe with them. He was impressed and enamored by the ginger-haired bounty hunter.

Before Cee could say anything, the door to the library opened and a large man entered with Colin following close behind. The man walked with both grace and purpose. He was much taller than his counterpart, and his aged face was framed with streaks of gray running throughout. While he had salt and pepper hair, his dark beard did not seem affected by the aging process, containing no gray of its own.

"Hello again Branda-Lynn," the tall man said. "I am deeply saddened to have kept you in the dark about Colin, but it was for your safety."

Cee stepped forward. "Mr. Fenrir, my name is Caiaphas Cerberus. This is my brother, Theokritos and his wife, Panterra." As he introduced Theo and Panterra, he pointed to each. They bowed as their name was called, in a sign of respect to the elder god.

"Please, Cerberus brothers, it should be I who is bowing to you. Just because I am old does not mean the formality is necessary. As you know, I am Fenrir.

But outside these walls, I am Fenn. I am but a humble blacksmith living in what appears to be a crumbling castle with my apprentice, Sir Colin."

"But Fenrir, you are an ancient god, and a powerful one at that. Why are you hiding?" Panterra spoke first, saying what everyone else was thinking.

"Well, what a story that is. It all began after I met Colin and Branda-Lynn's mother," he said, leaning against a bookcase full of leather-bound books.

"Umm, Fenrir, can you call me Brandy? I don't use my formal name often, and it kinda sounds weird."

"Of course, my apologies, Brandy." Then he continued almost as if she had not spoken. "The story starts before I met your mother." Fenrir paused again, interrupted by something in his head. "But first, let's have some refreshments because my story is a long one if you are willing to listen."

Immediately, Colin stood and went through the door. After a while, he returned with a small cart full of tea, coffee, and light hors d'oeuvres. Colin began to pass out drinks and plates for food as Fenrir sat back in his armchair and returned to his tale.

***

During the Titan Wars, Fenrir had tried to maintain as much neutrality as possible. He made objects for both sides but nothing which could change the outcome of the war. He knew to do so would affect fate, and he trembled at the thought. To remain neutral would be more difficult, but it was the right course of action during the time of such turmoil.

One morning while walking the path between his home and his forge, he ran across a soul who had gained sentience. It, unfortunately, seemed confused and was not able to decide what to bind to. It was common during these times, and Fenrir had the innate ability to communicate with souls in their orb form.

"Soul, do not be frightened. I will not harm you. I can help guide you."

All of a sudden, he heard the chirping of a woman in his mind. She was going on about what she wanted to be, and what she wanted to do.

Fenrir stopped her and tried his best to explain what she was now becoming. He explained the process and how to connect with the element or object she wanted to bind herself to.

After the explanation, the orb roamed over the small stream and approached a line of trees he had planted near his home. Each time she stopped, Fenrir held his breath, hoping to witness the joining. He had only ever remembered his own reconnection to the earthly plane after death. So, to standby and witness it as it happened to someone else was a great honor. But each time the orb moved on.

Fenrir was ready to move on, having seen many souls wonder for hundreds of years before joining. However, as the orb roamed over the path near Fenrir, it was drawn to a stone wall as if being pulled by a magnet.

Fenrir watched as the orb melded into the stone. The wall crumbled as it transformed into the shape of a human. As she stepped forward, Fenrir was awestruck for the first time in his long life.

She was magnificent, but of average height and build. Her skin had a deep gray, earthy tone, but everything was overshadowed by her stunning red hair. Speaking in Fenrir's mind, she asked if she was complete.

He could not respond, and he was not quite sure. Each time a soul connected with an element, they gained powers. By joining together with the stone, she gained the ability to manipulate her newfound element. She had become an elemental or rock golem. However, Fenrir did not understand until long after why she had regained her physical form after the joining. Her will was so powerful that her image of herself was stronger than the stone's. All of the golems he had seen before were far more rock then human.

Fenrir called her the name she kept repeating as an orb, "Cybele, welcome back."

Her smile was electric as she not only recognized her name, but also his voice from when she was an orb. Cybele and Fenrir spoke about the elements of the past she could remember. Cybele soon showed she had the ability to make stone do as she requested.

Fenrir had never seen such a strong ability before and asked if she would be his apprentice. Not having had an apprentice before, Fenrir decided she would be a wonderful addition to his forge and his life. She remained a part of his life as both an apprentice and companion for many years before she decided it was time for her to move on.

After Cybele left, Fenrir took some time off from his forge to rethink what he wanted. Did he want to continue being the forger, or did he want more? He realized he needed the forge as much as the forge needed him. After his break, he returned to the iron and renewed his passion for creation.

He had become known by both Gods and Titans as a creator of power-fused gems and relics. Because of his morality and neutrality, he required his creations be used only for the betterment of all. He never wanted his labors to become weapons of war. Over the years, Fenrir often thought of Cybele. He understood why she left, but he was scared of what may have befallen her. Had she been sucked into the war that had racked the world? Was she even still alive?

One morning, Fenrir was working on a piece for a friend when he sensed a presence behind him. He was not expecting anyone, and he had not yet met anyone who could sneak up on him. Turning around slowly, all he saw was darkness before a voice came from the shadows.

"Great Fenrir, I am in need of a stone with specific powers. I was told you are the only one who could create such a stone. It is imperative that it is completed quickly. I will pay you for your time," the shadow said.

"I don't know who you are, but if you have heard of me, you know I don't charge for my creations."

"I had heard this but wanted to get it from you. No one works for free, or at least they shouldn't." The shadow had solidified into a man of Egyptian descent.

"I have a very specific request, that I believe only you can help me with. Are you up for the challenge?"

Fenrir was never one to let a challenge go unmet and agreed to the man's request without being fully aware of its ramifications.

***

Cee cleared his throat. "What did he want?"

Fenrir sighed. "That will come in time. For now, please let me finish my story?"

"I'm sorry," Cee said as Brandy elbowed him in the ribs at his rudeness.

***

Fenrir had created the stone for its intended purpose. However, as he made it, he began to understand just the depths of what it could do. When almost finished, he had another customer arrive. One that he had met before and could be the answer to his unasked questions.

The woman who walked through the door stopped his heart just as she had done so many years before.

"Cybele, what are you doing here?" Fenrir walked over and hugged the woman.

She returned the hug. "I need you to make three stones."

"Of course, anything for you. Can I ask why you need them?"

Cybele explained the stones and why. Fenrir immediately liked her idea and set about making them.

A couple days after Cybele had walked back into Fenrir's life, the shadow man returned and demanded his stone. Fenrir initially told him he did not have it ready because it was far more difficult than anything he had created before. The man had threatened Fenrir and then vanished.

Once Fenrir gained insight into the original stone's properties, he realized it was much to powerful. It was something that could affect the outcome of the Titan Wars. The man who had initially requested it could not to be trusted with such a powerful stone. Fenrir knew he needed to hide it where he would never know where it went. Looking over his workbench, his eyes rested on the three unique stones. Reaching down Fenrir replaced the middle stone of the same color with the one he had made for the shadow man.

When Cybele came for the gifts, he had bundled them up and explained to her the importance of the middle stone. Knowing she would never betray him, he felt at peace. When the man arrived days later, Fenrir gave him the stone originally created for Cybele. In turn, the man threw him a coin with his brand on it. Fenrir, finding money meaningless, threw it in a drawer on his worktable.

12

"So, you switched the stone that was originally going to go to the guy, with the stone for Cybele. Did he find out?" Brandy asked

"Yes, he did. When the stone didn't work, he became rather upset. In fact, he even hired my cousin, Vioarr, Odin's son to kill me. Vioarr and I grew up together, and after he gave me the heads up on what the man wanted, I faked my own death. Vioarr helped and no one was the wiser. So, I came to live here.

Everything was peaceful until I heard about the sale of Cybele's original stone. To ensure it did not fall into the wrong hands, I needed someone to travel to Egypt to acquire the stone. It was not like I could leave; If my identity was to be discovered, then I assume a bounty would be placed on my head once again."

"Wait, is the stone Colin and I purchased for you from Egypt the one you gave this 'shadow man'?"

"Yes Brandy. I had heard there was a brother and sister team who had an innate ability to find objects, especially objects holding power. I knew they would be perfect for the job. I hadn't yet realized just why they were so good."

"What do you mean by that?" Cee asked, placing his arm protectively around Brandy's shoulders.

Brandy looked at him with an 'I can handle myself' look and shrugged out from under his arm.

"Remember when I said I had helped an orb and what I said about the being who had returned from orb form? Her name was Cybele, who called herself a 'stone' witch. Years after I went into hiding, she found me and mentioned how she had had two children with a human. She was beginning to worry about their future and asked me to keep an eye on them. I tried, but was regrettably unable to do so as I couldn't leave the castle without risk of death. When you and Colin arrived, I knew immediately you were her children."

"Wait, you call yourself Fenn, and no one figured it out?" Theo spoke.

Fenrir just shrugged.

"Wait, I don't understand what that means." Brandy looked from her brother to Cee to Fenrir.

"Well, my dear, it that your mom is immortal, and means you and Colin are likely immortal. Being that she was not entirely human when she had you, her abilities would have carried to you. So you have abilities that most of the people around you don't. Even now, standing next to the Cerberus, you have abilities they don't possess. Though, they have many you don't, so I wouldn't push your luck around them." Fenrir chuckled at his own comment before continuing. "Usually, that means you can hear things others can't or see things that others don't. For Colin, it means he has the uncanny ability to manipulate the will of stone. Since you and him are twins, I assume you have the same ability–"

"We are not twins." Colin and Brandy said in unison.

"–I am pretty sure you are, maybe you should ask your mother. Anyways, back to my explanation. Some individuals have extraordinary fighting skills or the ability to speak multiple languages without much work."

At the comment about fighting skills, Cee and Theo looked at each other and nodded. Cee now knew how she had taken down those guards. No human should have been able to do that, and it had bothered Cee that Brandy had been able to do it alone.

"Well, do you have any other questions for me, or do you want to come see my forge?"

"Yes, Fenrir, I do," Cee spoke up. Motioning for Diego to move forward, Cee pointed to Diego's collar. "Is this one of the stones you made for Cybele?"

Fenrir leaned forward while at the same time Diego, being Diego, puffed out his chest and ran up to the outstretched hand of Fenrir. Bringing the collar and the stone closer to Fenrir.

"Don't be so eager," Theo said to the dog.

"I won't be able to tell for sure until we go to my Forge. If you will follow me." Fenrir stood and turned, dog and humans following behind.

"But—" Cee wanted to press about why his collar didn't work to bring Turk back, but Theo shook his head slightly, indicating they should wait until they were in the forge. Begrudgingly, Cee kept his mouth shut as he stood.

Colin was standing by the doorway as Fenrir and the group walked out of the library. As Brandy walked out, leaving Colin alone, he turned and followed them.

Leading them to a small wooden door, Fenrir opened it and stepped down into what was a narrow staircase made of stone. The stones on both sides of the staircase looked much older than the building, which from what Cee could gather was old itself.

As they descended, Cee began to worry about their safety (or Fenrir's security). He did not believe what Fenrir had said about no one knowing he was here. After all, they had found him without much of a problem. Cee was worried about the only exit being the small stone passage.

Once they got to the bottom of the stairs, another wooden door opened into a large cavern. Looking around, Cee compared the size of this cavern to the one back home where the gate was located. He figured it was slightly smaller, but no less impressive. In the middle, there was a stone forge with a wooden worktable encircling most of the it. The tools used by Fenrir were resting on the edge of where there was no worktable. Even from a distance Cee could feel the heat emanating from the forge.

"Can you take the collar off so I can see it?" Fenrir asked.

Both Theo and Panterra said no at the same time.

Fenrir looked up with a confused expression. "Why not?"

"Because we don't want what happened to Turk to happen to Diego," they again said together.

Fenrir held up his hand to stop the frantic couple. "What happened to this 'Turk'?" Fenrir asked, looking from Theo to Cee.

Cee stepped forward from the group and told Fenrir the story of when Brandy took the collar from Turk. As he explained, Brandy lowered her head. Fenrir nodded as Cee continued, and tears slid down Brandy's cheeks.

Brandy knew it was all her fault and she felt the guilt from that. She couldn't do anything to bring Turk back, but she wished she could. This was not the first time she regretted taking the damn bounty.

After Cee finished his story, Fenrir walked over to Diego. "It's okay. What happened to Turk won't happen to Diego here. I promise." Before Theo could stop him, he reached down and took the collar off.

Diego continued to sit there and looked back and forth between Theo and Fenrir with his tail wagging. Everyone held their breath, except for Fenrir as the seconds ticked by.

"I can't hear him anymore, but he didn't turn to stone," Theo said stopping in his tracks.

"Because he won't. When Cybele asked for me to make three stones, they all had the ability to meld two minds together. They were created specifically for you and your brothers in order to communicate with your companions. I used what I had available, so that is why they are three different colors. Also, Cybele asked if I could make them slightly different as they were for three different people. Knowing what I did of you three, I made the colors resemble your personalities. Theo's stone reflects his eyes, Jan's matches his personality of being calm, and I made Cee's to match the other stone.

Fenrir walked over to one of his worktables and turned on the light above it. Inspecting the gem, he nodded and walked back to Diego. Fenrir replaced the collar around his neck. "Can you hear him again, Theo?"

"Yes, I can. I can say it was peaceful bliss for those two minutes," Theo replied as Diego leaned on him hard enough to push him down.

"Okay, Diego didn't change to stone. So why did Turk?" Cee asked.

"Dear Cee, you received the stone which wasn't originally meant for you. It was the one I had created for the shadow man. Because of what he had originally wanted, the stone had similar, but additional, properties," Fenrir said as he leaned against the table.

"But what caused him to become stone? Was it because it was ripped off?" Cee was getting frustrated by the half answers from Fenrir. At that last comment, he heard Brandy suck in air, waiting for Fenrir's answer. He knew she was hurting, but he needed to know.

"No, it was not because the collar was ripped off. It was the specific stone that was in his collar. When you connected the collar to any companion, it does much more than Diego's here. It transforms their soul. Not in a way that is noticeable by the companion, or even by you, but it does. I never truly knew the extent until now."

The breath Brandy had been holding was slowly released as she realized it wasn't entirely her fault, but the explanation still didn't make her feel any better.

"Why didn't previous companions turn to stone then?" Cee asked, even more confused than before. "If I replace the collar now, will Turk be okay?"

"Because you only took the collar off once the companion has passed. Therefore, there wasn't a living soul for the gem to consume or transform. Turk was very much alive when his collar was removed," Fenrir said, now looking around a nearby table. "To answer your question, no. I am sorry, but Turk as you know him is gone. Replacing the collar won't bring him back. The gem has consumed his soul."

"What the hell does that gem do then?" Brandy exploded.

Fenrir took a deep breath. He had been debating whether or not to tell them the full truth. It was, but also wasn't, his proudest moment. His only solace was his choice to turn the stone over to Cybele. He knew he could trust her, and that she would never willingly give the stone to someone who would use it for ill-intent.

"It does more than allow for communication between owner and companion. It also allows for communication between realms," Fenrir finally said.

"You mean like between the living and the dead?" Panterra perked up at his comment. A device like this could cause her Reapers issues if family members started speaking with reaped souls.

"No. Well maybe, but that wasn't its intention. The intention was not the dead, but rather the imprisoned."

Panterra felt slightly reassured, but knew the other shoe was about to drop.

Since no one caught on to what Fenrir was trying to say, he continued.

"It isn't the cross-realm communication that is specifically troubling. It's the fact you can communicate with those currently imprisoned in the furnace."

"Wait, someone from our realm can speak to the Titans? As in the ones who are chained? I remember being in there, and no one could talk to the outside world, not even the jailers," Panterra said, looking at Theo before continuing, "In fact, I tried for many years and there was nothing."

"It isn't like a speakerphone but given the right individual and right circumstances, I know it can communicate between our realm and the Furnace." Fenrir scoffed at the idea his creation wouldn't work as he said it did.

"Let me get this straight. You made a stone. During the Titan Wars no less. Which would allow someone to communicate with the banished? Did you even think about what you were doing?" Cee looked at Theo then back to Fenrir, the shock evident on his face. Cee thoughts returned to the war, and his hands started to shake.

"Cee, calm down. We can work with what we have," Brandy reached for his hands when she noticed his shaking.

"Now we have that out in the open, yes, I did create it. I was being egotistical, or maybe I was seeing if it could even be done. There was a good reason I didn't give it to him. I quickly realized what the ramifications could be. And since I was neutral during the war, I wasn't about to help him keep the war going, or gods forbid, start another one. When the war was raging, it was bad. Bad for everyone. They were dark days for sure, and I didn't want to go back to that."

Cee spoke up, "And you said you were neutral during the war? We trusted you. Hell, we protected you. But it seems like the war was very profitable for you after all."

Fenrir glared at Cee, but otherwise ignored the comment.

"I have a feeling someone knows about the stone." Brandy looked up at Fenrir.

"Why do you think that? No one knows about the stone aside from the individual who asked for it and your mother." Fenrir's face showed concern.

"Oh, maybe because when I took the bounty for Jan, I was told the dog would be an issue. But I could counter that by removing the collar, in fact the individual I spoke to said that it would cut the individual dog from its owner. There are Underworld

126

guards who, not only found my family's secret storage locations, but also stomped through it, taking Gods know what. Oh, and then I was attacked at my home, by likely the same Underworld guards. At least those will not be coming after me or mine anymore. I have a missing brother, and my Da is dead. So please tell me how someone doesn't know what is going on? You have a mole, or worse, maybe you are talking to people."

Even after being accused, Fenrir calmly turned towards Colin. "Did you know your father is dead?"

Colin looked at Brandy before answering. "No, but I assumed he was. I came to you after Brandy had been taken by the green lady and this one." He motioned toward Panterra. "Or at least someone who looked like you."

"We did take your sister, but not until after she broke into my house and stole something of my family's." As Panterra spoke, she grabbed Theo's hand.

"Brandy! What did you do? You really stole from the Cerberus? Why would you do that? They're the good guys." Colin broke character.

"Colin, before you start talking shit, I didn't know who they were at the time. Da finally gave me the go ahead to do my own bounty. So, naturally, I went to the bounty board in Dublin and found the bounty for Jan. I didn't know who they were. I contacted the number on the bounty and spoke to a man with a Middle Eastern accent. He told me yes, the bounty was still active. He also gave me the tip about the dogs, and how the collars held special powers which helped the brothers. I now know differently, but I didn't at that point," she said, almost throwing a tantrum.

When Brandy finished, Colin hit his forehead with the palm of his hand. "You are my sister, but seriously, you don't listen at all. You started this."

Brandy looked confused. "How did I start this whole thing?"

"By taking the job. It set into motion the chain of the events. However, it's not entirely your fault. It was fated to happen. I knew that, which is why I had you and Colin get the gem from Egypt. That way if the original one was stolen from the Cerberus, I would have the replacement needed." Fenrir said, calmly settling everyone.

"Did you know about the soul transformation properties of the stone?" Cee asked incredulously.

"No, some of the items I create have hidden powers that are unknown, even to me. But with this one, I knew there was more to it. Which is why I did my best to hide it."

"Why didn't you just destroy the stone? Problem solved," Theo questioned.

The only answer was a look of disgust from Fenrir. The silence that extended after that question left an opening for Brandy to consider what happened with her brother.

"What happened to you, brother?" Brandy looked over to Colin.

"After you disappeared, I went to the message center. You know, the one the bounty hunters use as a communication center?" Colin elaborated when he saw

to the group, he showed them the coin with a brand on it. "Where did you get this?" he questioned Fenrir.

Fenrir glanced over Cee's shoulder at the coin. "Oh that? That's the coin that was flipped to me by the shadow man. The one who ordered the stone you have here in the collar. I'm sure you have seen it, since you work with the Underworld daily." Fenrir stated, not sounding interested in the development.

"This symbol of a misshaped lion with a mane of snakes was on the chest plates of the Underworld guards Brandy killed at her house."

Fenrir seemed more interested now in Cee's response.

"Well, that is interesting. But let's get on with it. I have stuff to do, people to see, you know," Fenrir replied turning back to the collar. As he worked on replacing the stones, the group spoke about what they think happened to Oran, Brandy and Colin's eldest brother, as well as what their plans were for after they left.

"Okay, all done. Now Cee, this collar will react in the same way you had been using the other one. You will be able to communicate with your companions. Now, I will do something I should have done a long time ago. My ego got the best of me, and I could not bear to destroy something I had made. I am older and much wiser now, and realize that this much power should not be loose, regardless of who holds the power." Fenrir brought his massive hammer over his head to bash the stone. Cee didn't even know the man had the hammer. It was almost as if it appeared.

"You will not destroy that stone, wolf man." A voice floated in from the stone stairs.

"I don't know who you are, but I created it, and it is mine to destroy it!" Fenrir brought down his hammer with tremendous power, smashing the table in half and demolishing anything in its path.

Cee knew he had missed his mark. The soft breeze that picked up when the hammer fell was the reason. Cee might not have been a fighter, but his eye was quick. Whoever it was had covered the distance from the door to them with incredible speed. He could not see features, but the speed was amazing. The stone had been taken from under the hammer before its power could strike. Fenrir looked up and growled, knowing the stone had not been destroyed.

The group looked around as Fenrir stepped toward the door. As soon as he moved, the room began to flood with armored men. They all wore the same crest on their chests as the coin, which rolled across the floor as Cee dropped it. On quick count, Cee numbered 20 guards all surrounding the one individual with the stone in hand.

"Who are you to barge into my home and take something from me?" Fenrir said under a rising growl.

"I have a message from my master." The man turned, his face hidden by a hood. "He sent me to pick up what he paid for."

"What? You will just take it and leave? That is not very neighborly, fellow Underworlder," Theo mockingly stated.

Still unable to see the figure talking, the brothers and Panterra shifted into defensive positions, surrounding Fenrir.

The figure took a step back into the crowd. "We had hoped to use your skills again for what is to come, but it seems you have chosen a side this time. Master will be disappointed to learn you died in battle."

"Who is 'Master'?" Cee yelled at the figure.

"In time, in time. You will meet him," were the last words spoken as the being vanished up the passage.

"Well, this should be interesting." Theo had already produced his dual blades. Panterra had her scythe held high above her head, the light reflecting off the blade.

Even Brandy had produced a short sword and dagger when she stepped in front of Cee.

Cee began to argue, stepping to be in front of Brandy.

"Cee, don't try to protect me. I can protect myself." She turned and looked him in the eyes. "I have grown to realize you are not a warrior. It's okay, I have been trained to fight. Please stay back and be safe," she said, looking down at the sword in her hand before she leaned in and gave him a kiss.

Fenrir regained his position in the front of the group, hands wide, with long looking claws growing from his fingertips. "We must get the gem back."

Diego hunched and slipped away from the group disappearing into the shadows of the room.

The soldiers attacked in one large group. Each holding a short sword, blades glistening in the flickering light of the cavern. They covered the distance in moments and clashed with the small group.

Panterra's scythe ripped through the air as it crashed down into the first soldier within her range. The warrior fell motionless to the floor.

Theo, however, was not faring as well. Half of the group had focused on him, and he had a small dagger protruding from his leg. His swords blurred as they moved faster and faster, clashing again and again against the blades and armored bodies of his assailants.

One by one they fell. One of the soldiers sidestepped a glancing blow and stabbed out a quick killing blow. Before it could land, a large creature slammed into the unaware man, throwing him across the room. Diego followed, cutting the cries short.

The remaining soldiers threw themselves at Brandy, who was standing in front of Cee with Colin at her side. Slowly, the soldiers pressed the group, pushing them back against the furnace. Brandy had her hands full with a larger than usual soldier who seemed to know her every move.

Colin was fluent with a blade, but Cee knew he was not going to last much longer. Abandoning Brandy, Cee ran over to Colin, grabbing his attacker just as Colin lost his sword. Cee landed his fist hard across the Underworld guard's jaw, dropping him to the floor. The only movement was his faint breathing. As Cee realized what he had done, he heard a scream from the other side of the room. He turned to look and saw blood running down a gash on Brandy's side.

She stumbled backwards, grabbing the wound. Cee lost sight of her as another figure rushed him, sword out.

Brandy stepped back, gaining her balance while looking down at the blood flowing over her hand. The pain filled her with anger, anger that someone had gotten so close. She looked up and found her enemy taking off his helmet and revealing his face. "Oran? Why? What are you doing?" she said, surprised to see her brother.

"I chose to become stronger. Stronger than you, at least. And I found a master who would show me the way," he said dropping the helmet which clanged as it hit the ground.

"But you are my brother. We are family," she said, still shocked.

"You were always stronger. The pride and joy of our father. The one who could always see things that I could not. I would not allow some half breed to best me. I knew you would not understand, nor did our father," he said with a smile creeping across his face.

Realization grasped her like a cold hand. "You killed father!" She jumped him. The dagger flew from her hand, easily deflected by her brother. She knew he was stronger than when they last dueled. As she continued to lose ground from his sudden counterattack, she searched for help. Looking around, she knew the others were busy and could not help her.

Panterra had lost her weapon and was in a hand to hand battle with two soldiers. Theo had finished off most of his attackers and was moving to Panterra's side, passing one of his swift blades to her. Cee and Colin were nowhere to be seen, and both Diego and Fenrir were busy with assailants.

Brandy knew she was alone and backed into a corner with stone walls on both sides. She closed her eyes and willed the room to speak to her. It had worked before in the bounty trove; it should work here, she hoped. Breathing slow, she could feel the stone, and she knew where the stone fissures were. All of a sudden, there was a warmth filling her and expanding throughout the room. Opening her eyes, she reached out with her mind and tore a large stone from the wall. She sent it crashing into her brother's face, ripping his cheek and sending blood flying. Again, and again, she lifted the stones and twisted their will to hers.

Oran stood bleeding, sword still in hand, looking at her sideways. "It seems you have more surprises than I thought." He lifted the blade and rushed her, ignoring the stones. When he was close enough, he swung his blade intending to kill her. As it came down, it clanged off a stone shield that appeared between him and Brandy. Shocked by the shield, he did not notice the small blade until it pierced his chest, straight into his heart. As he fell the room became silent.

Brandy looked around and saw Cee running to her. She collapsed into his arms.

"Brandy, Brandy." Colin limped over, looking at the wound.

"She will be ok. The wound is not life threatening, but I fear mine is." Colin stumbled and joined the lifeless bodies on the floor.

Fenrir, now returning to his human form, ran over, lifting Colin from the other bodies. "Noooo! I am sorry, Cybele. I am sorry." He cried as he held the young man.

Fenrir's cry brought Brandy back to reality. She saw Fenrir, her brother, and Cee who was looking down at her, worried. She smiled briefly at him as the rest of the group came closer. As the group came closer, Brandy noticed a silhouette that was different. One that was familiar. In fact, a woman who looked like her. "Mother?" Brandy said softly. The whole group looked to the newcomer.

Through tears, Cybele answered, "Yes, my dear. But right now, we don't have time to talk, you need to rest." Looking briefly at Cee, she turned toward the Fenrir. "I have to help him, and I don't know how he will react to it. Cee, take her somewhere safe. Be safe my child, I know that I haven't been there in the past, but that is going to change. From now on I will be there for you." With that, Cybele touched the stone wall and a door slide up.

As soon as the door rose, the group could hear more enemies coming from the previously empty passage. Not waiting for an invitation, Cee grabbed Brandy, who had just stood up.

Panterra and Theo linked hands. The foursome, with Diego behind them, passed through the new portal. Looking back once, Brandy saw Fenrir and Cybele embrace before they turn toward the approaching horde.

***

Looking around the house, Cee wondered what the future held for him. He knew he had to let Turk go, and his loss of a companion paled in comparison to what had happened to Brandy.

She went from being a happy, young bounty hunter to a nearly orphaned half-god. She killed one of her brothers and her other one died right next to her. Now, none of them knew the status of her mother, but optimism was running low. Cee was glad Brandy had decided to return to Oregon with them. Her physical wounds were not serious, but emotionally, she was a wreck.

"So, what will you do now?" Cee nervously asked Brandy, who was standing with her eyes fixed on the statue of Turk.

"I don't know. I have never been in a place where tomorrow seems so dark," she said without averting her eyes.

"Brandy, I would like for you to do something for me. Well two things, but the first is about Turk."

She looked at him questioningly.

"Turk, he does not belong here. His favorite place was overlooking the falls and waiting for the next charge. Can you help me move him to the falls?"

She nodded in understanding. Cee left the room while Brandy faced the stone. She closed her eyes, small lines on her forehead appeared as she concentrated on the stone. Slowly, the stone stood and slowly walked from the room.

The stone dog led them to Cee's vehicle where he was ready with the door open. Like so many times before, Turk jumped into the front seat and sat motionless, waiting for Cee to buckle him in, waiting to go to work. Brandy climbed into the back seat and waited for Cee to start the engine. Cee looked at the magnificent dog and remembered all the times they had made this trip.

After a short drive, they arrived at the gates. They walked to the polished stone where Turk had loved to wait.

"Here, Brandy. He should be remembered in a place where he was happy."

Tears filled her eyes as she willed the stone to move again. Turk sat with regal authority facing the flowing water.

"Goodbye old friend," Cee whispered, and once again the stone became stationary.

Cee looked up to see Brandy, tears filling her eyes again. Reaching out to him, she grabbed his hand.

13

A month later

Cee walked into his room with a coffee. "Want to go shopping with me?"

"Sure, what are we shopping for?" Brandy said.

"A new companion. It's time. I also think Diego is getting tired of going to work twice every three days," Cee said sipping his coffee.

"Are you sure? Isn't that something you usually do with your brothers?" Brandy asked.

"Yes, but this time I want to go with you. I care about you a lot and want you to join me."

Brandy stood up wearing only a robe, which waved with the motion and she took the coffee from him. "What was that? You want to do what?"

"Really? I need to say it again?" Cee said and rolled his eyes.

"Yes, I like the sound of it when you say it. Please, for me?" Brandy said as she approached him.

Running his hands inside her robe, Cee wrapped his arms around her waist. "I care about you a great deal, Branda -Lynn."

"We can shop in a little while." She let her robe fall to the floor as she kissed Cee.

***

"I think I want a cat this time," Cee told his brothers later that day. "Brandy and I went shopping for a new pup, and I didn't really connect with any of them."

Theo shook his head.

"Well, this wouldn't be the first time, so I don't see why not. What type? Like a cougar or a bobcat?" Jan asked.

"No, I was talking to the director of the Wildcat Ridge Sanctuary about a large cat that would be a good pet, and they suggested I not get a cougar or anything wild. Way too many are already in the pet trade."

Theo interrupted, "We aren't in the normal pet owner's category either."

Without missing a beat, Cee responded, "Also, they would likely eat Diego and Jade, and we don't want that."

The three brothers looked over at the couch full of fur, where two snorts could be heard.

"So, don't they have bigger hybrids that are still pets?" Jan asked.

"There are and they have a lot of them there, but the issue is they are still partially wild. We have not had a wild animal in a long time. I don't want to add more complications to our lives than we already have."

"I agree, Cee. I think you should go for a domestic cat." Brandy had walked into the conversation with Panterra who had just returned from shopping in downtown Hood River.

"Ooooh, you should get a Maine Coon," Panterra suggested. "They're huge cats with huge paws, but they are also domestic. In fact, we noticed a poster advertising a new litter of Maine Coons across the river just the other day. I took a picture of it, thinking you may be interested in a kitty." Panterra grinned as she rattled off the numbers.

Cee wrote the number down and called it. "Hello, I saw your advertisement about a litter of Maine Coons. Uh huh, okay, yes. We could today. Thank you." Cee hung up and then turned to four eager faces. "So, they had 8 kittens, all of them are still available. They are 8 weeks old and can come home whenever. The owners have both parents on site and are available to show the kittens."

Brandy jumped up and down a little. "Yay we are getting a kitten."

"It's a working cat, if we end up getting one." Cee pursed his lips at her, while still smiling slightly.

"Yeah, because Diego and Sammy are such working dogs," Brandy commented, pointing at the two dogs laying on the couches in front of the fire. Brandy watched as both dogs seemed to shrug at her comment. "Whatever you say, it will be a 'work cat'. Are we going to go see the kittens?" Brandy asked with glee in her eyes and clapping her hands.

"Oh, this is going to be fun, the stoic Cerberus and the high energy bounty hunter," Theo said right before he hid behind Panterra.

"Don't hide behind me. You make your bed, then you lay in it." Panterra stepped aside, leaving Theo out in the open.

"Actually, you lay in my bed as well, missy," Theo said sticking out his tongue at her.

"And with that, Brandy, let's go look at some kittens." Cee got up and walked toward the front door.

As they arrived in White Salmon, they met with the owner of the Maine Coons. Walking into the room with the kittens, Cee saw a black kitten laying by itself while the rest of them were all cuddled together. Thinking back to when he chose Turk, he was much the same way. However, he felt different this time, so he decided to look at the pile of kittens a bit more. One wa s laying on its side with a smile on its face, enjoying the cuddles from its siblings. The kitten was a blue gray color, and its stomach was slightly lighter than its back. Pointing to the kitten, Cee looked at Brandy.

"I want that one."

Reaching down, the owners picked up the kitten and handed it to Cee. Cee gently stroked the top of its head, and he heard the kitten start purring and wiggling closer to him. Cee looked up. "This is the one I want. You agree Brandy?"

Brandy reached out to take the kitten. It smelled her hands first and then put a paw into her hand. She closed her hand over the little paw. Brandy could have sworn it smiled as it closed its eyes and laid its head in Brandy's hand. "Yup, this is the one."

"Great, let me get the paperwork. I believe that one is a little female. We had been calling her Cleo, but you are more than welcome to change her name."

Brandy and Cee looked at each other before turning back to the owner. "No, we think that Cleo is a great name."

"Okay, who shall I put on the paperwork as the owners?"

"Put Cee and Brandy Cerberus," Cee said before Brandy could open her mouth.

Brandy looked at Cee in shock. "We are talking about this later," Brandy whispered to Cee.

Finishing up the paperwork, the owner handed over their copy while Cee handed over the payment.

After they put Cleo into the small carrier they had brought with them, Brandy carried her to the car while Cee finished up with the owners.

"We appreciate you seeing us so soon. We lost our last pet recently and were eager to get another one."

"No, thank you, Mr. Cerberus. I hope Cleo brings you and your wife company for a long time."

Cee smiled. "We do as well."

As Cee got into the driver's seat, he looked at Brandy. "I guess we need to go shopping for kitten stuff."

"Umm, back there, what did you mean by Brandy Cerberus? Last time I checked, that was not my last name."

"Oh, yeah. I had been thinking that when you are ready, we should talk about getting married. I mean it doesn't have to be now, or anytime soon. I just care about you and want you to be part of my life. I mean, if you are okay with it. I guess we need to shop for something else too. Like a ring."

Cee thought the squeal that came out of Brandy was going to cause him permanent hearing loss, but it made him smile to know she was as happy about the prospect of marrying him as he was.

"Oh, I am so excited. I can't wait to tell Panterra and Meredith."

Since the two had kidnapped Brandy, they had all become good friends.

***

Once they got home, Brandy ran to tell Panterra and call Meredith about Cee's non-marriage, marriage question.

Jan and Theo were talking in the kitchen when Cee walked in.

"Heard you were getting married," Jan said.

"Yeah thinking about it," Cee responded back with as much emotion as Jan had put into the question.

"Good for you, marriage is a great thing. I mean, I don't have to cook for myself anymore," Theo said a little too loudly.

"I heard that, Theo. You keep talking shit, and I'll make you start cooking," Panterra called from the other room.

Theo lowered his voice even more. "She wouldn't dare. She knows I would likely poison us."

"Have you put the collar on the kitty yet?" Jan asked.

"Yeah, we did right after we bought a collar. The one Turk had been using was a bit too big, at least for right now. It pays to have stone worker to make sure it fits." Cee went and picked up the carrier. Opening it, Cleo stepped out onto the counter. "Jan, Theo, meet Cleo."

The two brothers both reached out and let Cleo sniff them before she rubbed up against their hands, purring the entire time.

Theo chuckled when Cleo licked his fingers. "So, what does it sound like to have a cat in your head?"

Cee looked at Cleo before answering, "There is a lot of talk about toy mice and wanting to chase the toy feathers we bought her."

Jan and Theo chuckled as Cleo jumped off the counter and went up to Diego. Cee stepped forward to stop what may happen, when Theo held his hand up.

"If they don't like each other, we need to know now, not later."

Diego lifted his nose from his paws, and Cleo bonked his nose with hers before laying down between his legs next to his stomach. Sammy looked up for a minute and then laid back to next to the fire.

"Looks like they will be fine, don't you think?" Cee anxiously asked his brothers, worried about his new companion.

Before they could answer him, Brandy ran into the room with Panterra. "Meredith isn't answering her phone. It isn't showing her receiving text messages either. It always shows. Jan have you talked to her?"

"Last night I did, she said she was going out to a Dryad thing last night, but she would be back in camp this morning. Maybe they went out? Let me try calling the clan leader, Erato. She should know what's going on."

Jan grabbed his phone from the counter and walked to his wing of the house.

"When are you planning to have the wedding?" Theo asked Brandy.

"I don't know. I mean, aside from my mother, my family is now in this room, is here in Hood River. We left Colin on the floor, and I know Cybele said she would try to help him. Heck I don't even know if Cybele and Fenrir made it out of the fight." Brandy had been worried about both Fenrir and Cybele since they had to leave them in Ireland.

As the four of them talked, they didn't notice Jan's slow return.

Eventually, Brandy noticed Jan standing there. "Jan, what's wrong? Did you get ahold of Meredith?"

As if in a trance, Jan started to explain what happened, "No, and something happened to the group at the event. Erato didn't have all the answers. From what she told me, it doesn't sound good. I need to go to Siberia. I need to call Hades, and we need to figure out how we are going to manage the gate while I'm gone. Panterra, can you reach out to your contacts to see if there are any reaps of Dryads. Cee I need you to—"

Theo barely caught Jan as he passed out.

"You heard him, let's get going." Cee stood before reaching for his phone.

The End

Acknowledgements

We would like to thank both of our families for giving us the time to write this book. Five minutes here and there really add up.

We would also like to thank Melanie Marsh and Terry Journey for their editing skills. Without you two this would not be the book it is today.

Thank you, Phycel Designs, for the beautiful cover. It is perfect not only for this book, but for the series.

Thank you to the beta readers who were honest about what they liked and didn't like.

Finally, thank you to all of our readers who have been with us since Ancient Resurgence, and to all of the new readers. Without your support, we would not be able to write.

About Author

F.L. Journey is the pen name for two authors who have come together to write in a variety of genres they enjoy. Look for more short stories and novels in the future from them.

Follow us on Facebook, Goodreads, Bookbub, and Amazon. Look for announcements about the conclusion of the Cerberus Brothers series, The Jade Commander Series, which follows Jan and Meredith.

By signing up for our newsletter, you will be sent exclusive content that spotlight all of the characters from the Cerberus Brothers Series.

Facebook: https://www.facebook.com/FLJourney
Amazon: https://amzn.to/2S3cCb
Goodreads: https://bit.ly/30bl6By
Twitter: @FLJourneyWriter

Other books by Author

Ancient Resurgence Series

Ancient Resurgence: Daniel's Story

Ancient Resurgence

Cerberus Brothers Series

Cobalt Warrior

Crimson Scholar

Jade Commander (Coming 2024)

Matching Galaxies

Princess and the Pirate (Coming 2024)

Anthologies

Illusions – "Death Awaits" – July 2024

Little Witches – "Growing up Teen Witch" – October 2024

www.ingramcontent.com/pod-product-compliance
Lightning Source LLC
Chambersburg PA
CBHW032313310726
48973CB00008B/2630